RIBBON OF YEARS

Ribbon of Years

Robin Lee

HATCHER

Tyndale House Publishers, Inc.

WHEATON, ILLINOIS

Visit Tyndale's exciting Web site at www.tyndale.com

Be sure to check out Robin's Web site at www.robinleehatcher.com

Edited by Traci L. DePree

Designed by Melinda Schumacher

Scripture quotations are taken from the *Holy Bible*, King James Version.

The Scripture quotations contained herein are taken from the *Holy Bible*, Revised Standard Version, copyright © 1946, 1952, 1971 by the Division of Christian Education of the National Council of the Churches of Christ in the United States of America, and are used by permission. All rights reserved.

Scripture quotations taken from the *New American Standard Bible*, © 1960, 1962, 1963, 1968, 1971, 1972, 1973, 1975, 1977 by The Lockman Foundation. Used by permission.

Scripture quotations are taken from the *Holy Bible*, New Living Translation, copyright © 1996. Used by permission of Tyndale House Publishers, Inc., Wheaton, Illinois 60189. All rights reserved.

Library of Congress Cataloging-in-Publication Data

Hatcher, Robin Lee.
  Ribbon of years / Robin Lee Hatcher.
    p. cm.
  ISBN 0-8423-4009-2
1. Aged women—Fiction. 2. Auctions—Fiction. I. Title.
PS3558.A73574 R5 2001
813´.54—dc21   2001001171

Printed in the United States of America

07 06 05 04 03 02 01
9   8   7   6   5   4   3   2   1

To Sara Jones,
*   sister in Christ and in heart.*
*   Thanks for being an encourager in countless ways.*

Every time I think of you, I give thanks to my God.

I always pray for you,

and I make my requests with a heart full of joy

because you have been my partners

in spreading the Good News about Christ.

PHILIPPIANS 1:3-5, NLT

~

Ribbon of Years was born in my heart while I watched reports on television of a tragedy where innocent lives were lost through no fault of their own. As I watched the grieving families of those who died, I found myself asking, "How do people trust God to bring them through difficult things like this? How do Christians walk by faith, no matter what trials come their way?" God used so many people to give me answers to those questions and to help me develop this story until it became the novel you hold in your hand now. While I can't thank them all, I do want to thank a few.

To Pastor Gene Arnold, whose sermons, Sunday after Sunday, gave me the answers I needed even before I knew I had questions. Thank you, Gene, for your faithfulness in shepherding the people of Trinity Fellowship.

To George Hage, for sharing his heart with me and with others. George, I pray that I've been true in the way I used what you so freely gave.

To the members of the Trinity Women's Care Group, for challenging me, encouraging me, teaching me, praying for me.

To Christie Moore, for her obedience to minister to the nations, including to a small group of women in McCall, Idaho. Christie, may God bless you, indeed, and may He enlarge your territory.

To all the wonderful people at Tyndale House Publishers. You are too many to name, and the reasons for my thanks are too many to list.

JULIANNA

SUMMER 2001

WOULDN'T IT BE GREAT IF PEOPLE COULD BEGIN THEIR LIVES AGAIN, IF WE could get a clean slate? That's what I was thinking as I drove through a quiet Boise neighborhood on a warm Friday morning in August.

When I was a kid, we called that a "do over." I wanted a "do over" in life. Of course, I knew I wouldn't get one. You got what you got, and you might as well make the best of it.

Leland, my husband of twenty-four years, seemed content enough. So did Traci, our daughter.

But I kept feeling like there should be something . . . oh, I don't know. Something *more*.

At my age—forty-four this year—I thought I should know what life was about, but I didn't. It all seemed pretty futile. I only had to look at the newspaper headlines or listen to the evening news to confirm those feelings.

Leland knew I was at loose ends, restless, discontented. Poor man. He'd tried a dozen different remedies to lift my spirits, all to no avail.

I sighed deeply, my gaze fixed on the more-than-a-century-old homes, looking for my destination. In this part of town, the blocks were laid out in precise, orderly squares, the ancient trees gnarled, their roots buckling the sidewalks from the underside.

Spying the sign I was searching for—Estate Sale Preview Today, it proclaimed in large red letters—I pressed on the brake pedal and pulled to the curb.

I stared at the two-story Victorian-era house and sighed again. Normally I loved coming to these old homes and looking for that special find. But today . . . well, I doubted anything would interest me in my present mood.

"You're here," I muttered. "Make the best of it."

I grabbed my purse from the passenger seat, opened the door, and got out.

~

I was greeted on the front porch by an attractive young woman— twenty-something and ultrathin—in a white silk suit, the jacket long, the skirt short. She had legs that didn't end, straight blond hair cut in a Jennifer Aniston style, striking blue eyes, and a thousand-watt smile.

Not exactly the sort of girl who made a forty-something woman in an identity crisis feel good about herself.

"Welcome," she said as she handed me a brochure. "Feel free to browse. Everything in the house is for sale. If you have questions, ask one of the setup crew. The auction will begin tomorrow morning at ten."

"Thanks," I mumbled as I moved toward the open doorway.

The moment my foot fell on the parquet floor of the entry, I felt surrounded by the past. The paper on the walls was reminiscent of the 1950s, a pastoral scene on an off-white background with pale green trees, grazing sheep, and shepherdesses with hooped skirts and crooked staffs. The baseboard and wainscoting had been painted the same shade of green as that in the wallpaper. It made me think of my grandmother's house.

I paused, closed my eyes, and breathed in. Yes, it even smelled a bit like Grandma's house used to. A hint of rose petals. A little musty. A dash of old age and disuse.

I heard voices behind me and quickly moved forward. There

were more people in the living room off to my right, so after a
quick glance inside, I bypassed it, heading instead for the stairs.
I liked to do my antique browsing alone.

There were two bedrooms, a bathroom, and a small sitting
room on the second floor of the house. No one was in the sitting
room, so I went in and closed the door behind me.

It wasn't until I was inside that I realized the room seemed to
be set up for a meeting. An odd collection of chairs—a wooden
rocker, a love seat, a recliner, an upholstered wing-backed chair—
formed a circle around an oval coffee table. Atop the table was a
plain brown cardboard box, perhaps three feet by three feet in
size. I might not have paid any more attention if it weren't for the
green satin ribbon tied around the box.

I crossed the room for a closer look.

The top panels had been folded over one another rather
than being taped, and across one of those panels, someone had
written with a black marker: *My life.*

That was all. Just those two words, in large bold script. *My
life.*

Should I look? I wondered as I gingerly touched the box.

"She did say everything in the house is for sale," I answered
myself aloud.

That seemed justification enough to untie the ribbon and
see what was inside.

What I found was not momentous, as I'd hoped. It was
merely an odd collection of items, none of them of any apparent
value. A rolled-up poster. A tan-colored serving tray, the kind
used in cafeterias, only smaller; this one had been decorated with
stickers, glitter, and Bible verses. A soldier's service cap, faded by
time. A Nixon campaign button. A pair of gold filigree earrings.
A striking black-and-white photograph of a majestic mountain
range at either sunset or sunrise; it had been framed in black
wrought iron, and the glass was cracked in the lower right

corner. And finally, a soda-fountain glass, the kind they used to serve milk shakes in when I was a kid.

"So much for your life, whoever you are."

What would I put into a box marked "My life"?

Given the way I'd been feeling of late, that was a frightening thought. Except for raising my daughter, it didn't seem my life had accounted for anything.

The door to the sitting room squeaked open, revealing an elderly man, stoop-shouldered, bald-headed, and leaning on a cane. He raised his bushy gray eyebrows when he saw me.

"Sorry, miss," he said in a papery thin voice. "I was told I'd find—" he stopped abruptly when his gaze settled on the open box. "There it is." He shuffled forward. "Miriam would sure be surprised if she knew I got here before the others. She always complained about me bein' late."

Miriam?

The man came to stand before me and stared inside the box. "My, oh, my. How'd she manage to hang on to that all these years?" He pulled the rocking chair close and sat down. Motioning with a quivering index finger, he said, "Hand me that poster, will you?"

I obliged, at the same time wondering how to gracefully make my escape. The curious sort I might be, but I knew some folks tended to talk at length about things that didn't interest me in the least.

The elderly gentleman unrolled the poster. I couldn't tell if he was about to cry or if his eyes were simply watery from old age.

"I was with Miriam the night she got this," he said. "Let's see now. That would've been about 1936, I reckon. Yes, that's when it would've been. I remember 'cause that was the same year I took a job at Tucker's Insurance. My father'd had a hard time after losing our farm. All of us living with his cousin, and he couldn't get a job. He needed my help."

What was I supposed to say to all that?

His gaze met mine. "Guess 1936 seems a long time ago to someone as young as you."

"I'm not all that young."

"Reckon that's what you think now. Time'll change that, same as it changed Miriam and me."

"Was she your wife?"

"Nope." He shook his head. "She wouldn't have me. Not in '36, and not later either."

Heaven only knew what possessed me to ask, "Why not?"

He didn't seem to hear me. He was staring at the poster, unrolled on his lap, his gnarled hands holding it in place, but his eyes had a faraway look in them. "She was fifteen that summer, prettiest girl in town and full of the dickens. When I think about some of the stunts she pulled, nothin' short of a miracle that she lived to see twenty, let alone eighty." He chuckled softly. "A regular spitfire, she was back then."

MIRIAM
SUMMER 1936

CHAPTER TWO

"ARE YOU CRAZY, MIRIAM?" JACOB MCALLISTER WHISPERED. "YOU get us caught, my dad's gonna take the hide right off my backside."

Miriam Gresham ignored him. Jacob was a worrywart. Worse than any old woman she'd ever known.

"Are you listening to me?" he persisted, his voice rising slightly.

"No." She continued to pry open the glass door that held the *Anna Karenina* publicity poster. The theater had another just like it inside the lobby. They wouldn't miss this one. "I'm not leaving without this poster. You know how much I adore Garbo."

"Enough to wind up in jail over?"

Miriam glanced at Jacob's shadowed figure and chuckled softly. It was one o'clock on a Wednesday morning. Main Street was black as tar on this moonless night.

"We're not going to get arrested," she assured him. "Officer Tucker doesn't go out on patrol again for another hour. And besides, if you'd showed up when you were supposed to, we wouldn't—"

"Any girl who knows the patrol schedule of the cops is trouble for sure," he grumbled. "I don't know why I hang out with you."

"So go home. I don't need you here. I can do this all by my lonesome." She went back to work, sliding the flat edge of the screwdriver under the lower right corner of the glass.

Miriam knew that, despite his complaining, Jacob wouldn't leave. He was sweet on her, and everybody in River Bluff knew it. She liked him, too, but not the way he wanted.

At seventeen, Jacob thought a lot about responsibilities and family and settling down. Getting a job, getting married, having kids. Growing up and growing old, that was how Miriam saw Jacob's future, same as she saw it for most of her classmates.

But she wasn't ready for that. Not yet. She wanted to be an actress like Greta Garbo. She wanted to be in motion pictures. As soon as she could scrape together enough money for a ticket, she was taking the bus to California, to Hollywood, to MGM Studios.

With a loud *creak* the glass door on the display case came loose. She swung it to the side, then quickly plucked the thumbtacks from the four corners of the poster and snatched it from the corkboard.

Her pulse raced. "Okay, let's get out of here. Quick!"

Miriam darted around the side of the theater and down the alley. She knew Jacob followed right behind. She could hear the soles of his shoes slapping against the hard-packed dirt as they ran. Instinct rather than sight carried them through the darkened backstreet to where they'd parked her dad's Model T.

"Hurry up," she ordered Jacob as she scrambled into the automobile.

He went straight to the crank, their routine down to a science after a year of late-night escapades. When Miriam gave it any thought at all, she found it amazing that her parents hadn't discovered her absences.

Just went to prove what a great actress she was. Her folks didn't suspect a thing. They slept peacefully every night, trusting that their daughter wouldn't think of disobeying them.

If they only knew . . .

~

River Bluff, a small town by most any standard, was located about thirty-five miles outside of Boise, the state capital. It consisted of not much more than four streets—two running north-south and two running east-west—where one could find the police station, the Bluff Diner, one bank, five churches, the elementary school on the west end and the high school on the east end, a mercantile and a drugstore, Tucker's Insurance Agency, which was owned by Officer Tucker's Uncle Mooney, and the River Bluff Movie House.

The area farmers grew a little bit of everything—corn, onions, sugar beets, alfalfa, apples, cherries, grapes—on land that had been laboriously reclaimed from the desert; lava rocks had been cleared by hand, the rich volcanic soil watered from the miles and miles of irrigation ditches and canals that spiderwebbed out from the Boise and Snake Rivers.

Frank Gresham, Miriam's father, was the town druggist and an elder at the All Saints Community Church. His wife, Eliza, taught the first, second, and third graders at the elementary school and sang in the church choir on Sundays. Both Frank and Eliza were respected members of the town.

And both had a few blind spots when it came to their one and only daughter.

Not so, Officer Del Tucker. When Patrick Finch called to report a theft at the movie house, Tucker's first suspect was Miriam Gresham. Not that he'd caught her in one of her pranks. He hadn't. But he had an instinct about these things, and he figured it was about time she knew he had his eye on her and her shenanigans.

Del removed his hat as he opened the door to the Main Street Pharmacy. A tiny bell announced his arrival; ceiling fans whirred softly, stirring the warm air.

"Be right with you," Miriam called from the storeroom at the back of the building.

"No hurry," he returned as he strode down a narrow aisle, glancing at the shelves on either side of him.

When she appeared in the doorway, she flashed him a confident smile, not the least bit troubled to see him. "Good afternoon, Officer Tucker. What can I do for you?"

Nobody should be that sure of herself at fifteen.

"Is your father around?" he asked.

Del already knew the answer. Frank Gresham went home for lunch every day at this time. During the school year, he closed the store for the noon hour. But when summer months arrived, ever since she turned twelve, he'd let his daughter tend the cash register and wait on customers.

"He's at lunch," Miriam said.

"Is it that time already?" Feigning surprise, Del looked at his watch.

"Is there something I can get you?"

He shook his head. "Actually, I need to ask him how late he worked last night. Do you happen to know?"

She widened her pretty blue eyes. "He came home at the usual time. He didn't come back to the store after supper as far as I know."

"Well, tell him there was trouble over at the movie house after it closed last night. I need to know if he saw anything unusual before he left." He gave her a hard look. "You remember to tell him that, will you?"

Miriam didn't even blink. "I'll remember, Officer Tucker." Sugar wouldn't melt in her mouth, she looked so sweet. "I hope it wasn't anything serious."

"It was, if you call taking something that's not yours serious."

"Something was stolen?"

She asked the question with such complete innocence, Del was nearly convinced he was wrong about her involvement.

"How dreadful," she added. "Was it something valuable?"

Nearly convinced but not quite.

"Not particularly." He placed his hat back on his head. "But I don't take kindly to thieves, no matter what they've stolen."

~

Miriam may have looked as cool as a cucumber the whole time Officer Tucker was standing on the opposite side of the counter, but inside she was a sorry sight, a mass of tension and screaming nerve endings. There was something about those brown eyes of his. He seemed to see straight into her soul.

She was mighty glad when he left the store.

And none too soon. No more than two minutes later, her dad entered through the rear door. "I'm back, pixie," he said as he hung his hat on the coatrack, then removed his suit jacket. "Any calls?"

"No." She pursed her lips, debating whether or not to "forget" Officer Tucker's visit. "No calls."

Best not to forget, she finally decided.

"Officer Tucker was in a while ago. He said something was stolen over at the movie house last night. He wanted to know if you saw anything before you left."

"Not a thing." Her dad shook his head. "What's this town coming to?"

Miriam felt a flush rise up her neck and into her cheeks. She turned away and wiped the counter with a rag. She didn't want to meet her dad's gaze.

There wasn't much that bothered Miriam Gresham, but disappointing her dad was one thing that did. She was his pixie, his precious angel girl. He told her so all the time. Whenever anything was wrong, she could count on his warm embrace and abundant love.

On the other hand, he was a bit of a fuddy-duddy. He was forever and always trying to teach her some lesson. More likely than not, that lesson would be sprinkled with words from the Good Book. All well and good, she supposed, for somebody her dad's age. At forty, he didn't have much choice but to walk the straight and narrow. All his good years were behind him.

But Miriam's life lay before her like one huge banquet. She wanted to taste it all. There'd be time enough for religion when she got old.

"Caught you," her dad said as his hand fell upon her shoulder.

Guilty heat flared in her cheeks again as she turned to look at him.

"You weren't listening to a thing I said, little daydreamer."

"Sorry, Dad."

He grinned. "Go on. Your lunch is waiting, and your mother will be wondering where you are."

"Are you sure you don't need me to do something else?"

"I'm sure." He kissed her cheek. "Besides, you're supposed to take your brother swimming this afternoon."

Miriam groaned. She'd completely forgotten her promise to Arledge.

Her dad laughed. "It's not going to hurt you to spend a little time with him. You've only got the one brother. Be good to him."

"I try, Dad, but he can be such a . . ." She sought for an appropriate word that she could use with her father, finally settling on ". . . brat."

"So can you," he said affectionately.

Miriam groaned again as she headed for the door, knowing there was no point in delaying the inevitable. Like it or not, she was stuck with Arledge for the afternoon.

CHAPTER THREE

When Robert McAllister lost his farm to the bank in '33, he and his family were taken in by a cousin, Orland Bruce. All five of the McAllister boys had been sharing an attic bedroom ever since.

While Jacob loved his four younger brothers, there was such a thing as too much togetherness. So he could sympathize with Miriam when she complained about having to look after twelve-year-old Arledge.

Still, swimming seemed like a good idea on a day that was turning into a scorcher. Especially when it afforded him the leisure of looking at Miriam in a bathing suit. She was definitely an S.Y.T.—a Sweet Young Thing. The prettiest girl in River Bluff. Probably the prettiest in the whole county.

"Arledge, you get over to this side right now!" Miriam hollered at her brother without lifting her head from the sun-drenched rock where she lay on her back, her golden blonde hair fanning out like a halo. "You know Mother doesn't want you getting so far out."

"Ah, sis. I'm not a baby."

"You mind me. You hear? I'm not getting in trouble with Dad because of you."

Jacob chuckled. If that wasn't rich, he didn't know what was. There was Miriam, worried about getting into trouble because Arledge swam too far from shore, but she hadn't been afraid to break into the theater's display case last night and steal that stupid movie poster!

"Jacob," she said, her eyes closed again.

"Hmm?"

"Why don't you come with me to California? Why don't we go now, this summer?"

His heart skipped a beat. "Are you proposing to me, Miriam?"

She released an unladylike snort. "Of course not, you idiot." She sat up and looked at him. "I just don't see any reason for me to waste time finishing high school. An actress doesn't need a diploma. She needs talent, and I've got that. If you could get your hands on a car—"

"*I'm* the idiot? It's more than a car we'd need. We'd need money for gas and food and a place to stay. In case you haven't noticed, most of the country's outta work."

"Well," she said with a sigh, "there's got to be some way to get to Hollywood before I'm too old to become a star. Besides, I'm going to die if I'm stuck in this place much longer. Simply die." She lay down, rolled onto her stomach, and turned her face away from him.

Jacob stood and walked to the swimming hole's edge.

From the first time he'd laid eyes on Miriam—when she was all of six and Jacob was eight—she'd owned his heart. He remembered that warm summer morning as if it were yesterday. He'd come into town with his dad to get supplies for the farm, and there'd been Miriam, skipping rope on the sidewalk outside the drugstore. When she noticed him watching her from the bed of the pickup truck, she'd grinned, never missing a beat with the rope.

He didn't know if it was her dimples that got to him or the twinkle of mischief in her eyes. All he knew was, from that moment on, he was a goner.

He frowned. Maybe he *should* try to find a way to take Miriam to California, he thought as he stared at his reflection in the water. Maybe if he did something as dramatic as that, she'd think of him as more than her childhood pal. Maybe then she'd realize that he'd become a man.

Besides, what would he be leaving if he did go? It wasn't as if he was college-bound, now that the farm was gone. He'd have to take that part-time clerking job he'd been offered with Mooney Tucker, maybe eventually become an insurance salesman.

An insurance salesman. He didn't have to be told that Miriam wasn't going to marry one of those. Leastwise, not if she knew about it first. She wanted excitement and glamour. She wasn't about to settle for ordinary.

And nobody was more ordinary than Jacob McAllister—six feet tall, lanky and rawboned, freckle-faced. The only thing *not* ordinary about him was his carrot red hair with matching eyebrows, and that wasn't exactly a plus.

Nobody was more broke than Jacob either. The whole McAllister clan hadn't more than a few nickels to rub together at any one time. It grated on Jacob, although he tried not to let it show. He knew their current circumstances were plenty hard on his dad's pride without Jacob adding to his troubles.

'Course, maybe if he left town with Miriam that would help his folks. One less mouth to feed, after all.

But he knew he wouldn't go. Not even for Miriam. He had to take that job at Tucker's Insurance.

Feeling suddenly frustrated and angry, Jacob dove into the water and swam to the opposite end of the pond.

~

Poor Jacob, Miriam thought, watching him through half-closed eyes. *If only he could understand.*

She didn't mean to hurt him, but neither could she help it that she didn't return his feelings. She knew he was waiting until she was a little older before he really and truly asked her to marry him. If that happened, she would have to turn him down and break his heart. She hoped to be long gone from River Bluff before then. Jacob was nice enough, as boys went, but when the day came for Miriam's wedding, she planned to marry a famous movie actor, not the son of a farmer.

She closed her eyes and envisioned Garbo as Anna Karenina. When Miriam fell in love, it would be with that sort of passion. It might even be with that sort of tragedy.

She pictured herself in black and white, moving across the silver screen, stepping into the embrace of a handsome leading man, this one bearing a striking resemblance to Clark Gable. She waited to feel the touch of his lips upon hers, to experience her first kiss, to—

Cold water cascaded down upon her, drenching her from head to toe.

With a shriek, she jumped to her feet. "Arledge Francis Gresham! I'm going to skin you alive!"

~

Frank Gresham looked up from his account books when he heard the jingle of the bell over the front door. "Afternoon, Mooney." He removed his reading glasses and rose from his chair.

"Afternoon, Frank. I came to pick up those pills Doc Carson wants Theodora to take. You got them ready?"

"Sure do." He reached for the bottle. "Want those on your account?"

Mooney nodded, then removed his hat and wiped his forehead with his shirt sleeve. "It's a hot one today. Gard said it was over ninety degrees at noon." He glanced upward. "Smart thing, having those ceiling fans. Could use a few of 'em over in my office."

"They're a lifesaver in the summer."

"Did Del tell you about the theft at the movie house last night?"

Frank handed the small bottle of pills to Mooney. "Not personally. He came into the store while I was home for lunch. But he told Miriam and asked if I'd seen anything out of the ordinary." He shook his head slowly. "A real shame. Used to be things like that didn't happen in River Bluff."

"Well, Del's sure to catch the culprits, sooner or later."

"I hope so. And I hope when he does that their parents give them a sound licking."

Mooney agreed, exchanged a few pleasantries, then said, "Better get this medicine home to Theodora." He waved farewell as he left the store.

Thinking about Mooney's ailing wife, Frank pondered his owned blessed state as he closed out the register for the day and locked up the cash. Eliza was beautiful and kind, and his children were healthy and well behaved. Other than the occasional sibling squabbles, Miriam and Arledge were as close as any he'd known. Without a doubt, God had been good to the Gresham family. Sure, times had been hard since the crash. Business in the drugstore was down, and some folks couldn't pay their bills. Others had lost their homes and farms, and had been forced to move away. But Frank was confident the Lord would bring them through.

Yes, indeed, Frank Gresham was a blessed and contented man.

He checked the back door to the alley before removing the white coat he wore at the store and replacing it with his regular suit coat. Then, keys in hand, he headed for the front door. It opened before he reached it.

"Hi, Dad."

"Hi, pixie. Did you come to walk home with me?"

"Sure did." Miriam's grin revealed dimples in both cheeks.

"Have a good time swimming?"

She shrugged. "It was okay."

They stepped outside, and Frank locked the door. When he turned, he found Miriam gazing toward the movie theater.

"You might as well forget it," he said with gentle firmness.

"But, Dad—"

"Sorry, honey. That film isn't appropriate for a girl your age. Maybe not for any age."

"But, Dad, Leo Tolstoy is considered one of Russia's greatest nineteenth-century novelists. *Anna Karenina* is a classic. Just ask Mrs. Yancy, my lit teacher."

Frank considered his words before replying. "Tolstoy's novel may very well be great literature, Miriam, and it may also be a classic. But the story's heroine makes many misguided choices. The kinds of choices you don't need to read about at your age."

"I'm not a child, Dad, and I know what the story's about. Anna commits adultery and later she kills herself." She rolled her eyes. "I guess she was a biff at both love and life."

"A what?"

"A biff. You know, a loser."

"Never judge others too harshly, pixie, for as we judge so are we judged."

"It's a book, Dad."

"No, it's an attitude of your heart. I want you to learn about love from the source of love Himself. They rarely portray real love on the movie screen."

She sighed as dramatically as any fifteen-year-old could, as if to say, *I know, Dad.*

Frank reached out and took hold of his daughter's hand. "You've only just begun your life, Miriam. I want you to live it well."

"I plan to," she answered, a jaunty twinkle in her eyes.

O Lord, watch over my beloved girl.

CHAPTER FOUR

IF MIRIAM HAD HER DRUTHERS, THE GRESHAM FAMILY WOULD
attend a church with a bit more pomp and circumstance than
All Saints Community. The choir didn't wear satin robes. The
building didn't have stained-glass windows, and the pews didn't
have padded seats like the Catholic church down the street.
Even the altar area was ordinary—just a black leather Bible and a
simple wooden cross on a table behind the pulpit from which the
minister delivered his sermons.

On this particular Sunday morning, Miriam fanned herself
as she watched the sweat bead on Pastor Desmond's forehead,
then trickle down the sides of his beet-red face. Why didn't he
stop preaching and let them go home? It was hotter than all get-
out today. She could scarcely breathe, the air was so still.
Anybody with a lick of sense was sitting in the shade near the
river, cooling their feet in the water as it flowed by, not stuck in
a stuffy church.

She glanced at her dad, seated on the other side of Arledge.
It wouldn't have occurred to Frank Gresham to be anywhere
else than right where he was now, listening attentively. When
they walked home after church, Miriam knew he would discuss
the sermon with her mother, and while Eliza Gresham prepared
their Sunday dinner, he would open his Bible and make notes in
the margins, a thoughtful frown pinching the center of his forehead.

The sameness of it nearly drove Miriam insane.

If I don't get out of this town soon, I'll go mad. Stark raving mad.

But Jacob was right. She needed more than an automobile to get her to California. She needed money, and she needed help. She couldn't go alone.

Are you proposing to me, Miriam? Jacob's words echoed.

Would he take her to California if she promised to marry him? He might. Not that she would actually go through with it once they got there. She wasn't going to Hollywood in order to be Mrs. Jacob McAllister. Still, if it served her purpose . . .

Hmm . . .

She turned her head to the right, glancing over her shoulder, across the aisle, and two rows back. That was where the Robert McAllister family sat, right behind the Bruce clan.

Jacob was looking at her.

It only took meeting his eyes to know he'd go with her if she promised to marry him. He would do anything for her. He loved her. It was as clear as the nose on her face.

She straightened in the pew, trying to appear as if she were listening to the sermon, even as her thoughts continued to churn.

They didn't have a car, and there was no hope of getting one. So they would have to walk, get rides from other travelers, perhaps hop on a train. The tramps going back and forth across the country did it all the time. Why not her? She wasn't afraid. It would be exciting.

But they would still need money, not easy to come by in these troubled times. In her mind, she heard the *ka-ching!* of the cash register at the drugstore. A shiver ran through her.

It wouldn't really be stealing, she reasoned. *Not if I intend to pay it back.* She glanced toward her dad. *He'd give it to me if he understood how badly I want this. He'd help me if I was older. So all I'd be doing is moving things along a little bit faster. That's all. He'd see that in the end.*

Frank reached for the hymnal and rose from the pew. Miriam quickly did the same. He looked at her, and he smiled, then held the open hymnal toward her so they could each hold one side of the book. The gesture drew her closer to him, Arledge standing between them.

Her dad would be hurt if she left home. So would her mother. But they would forgive her, given time. They always forgave her. She could count on that, like counting on the rising and setting of the sun.

~

The All Saints Community Church choir had five members— two sopranos, one alto, a tenor, and a bass—plus the organist, Grace Finch. The same five people had made up the choir for the past decade. They wouldn't win any awards for their singing, but they were competent enough and enjoyed what they did.

Certainly that was true of Eliza Gresham. She felt closest to God whenever she sang. Although she held her hymnal in front of her, she had no need to look at the words of "Nearer, My God, to Thee." Instead, she gazed at her family and felt an overwhelming burst of thankfulness for them.

Eliza had fallen in love with Frank Gresham when she was all of sixteen. She remembered the day . . . June 1, 1917 . . . the hour . . . 2:15 P.M. . . . and the place . . . on the sidewalk at the corner of Main and Elm, right outside the mercantile.

Frank was a soldier, twenty-one, his parents deceased, and he was about to ship out with his company to fight in the Great War. He came to River Bluff with Mooney Tucker, a fellow soldier and friend.

Eliza lost her heart the moment she laid eyes on him, and nothing had changed about that in all the years since—except perhaps she loved him even more today.

They were married when Eliza was eighteen, and there hadn't been a day since then that she hadn't thanked God for sparing Frank's life in that horrible war, for allowing her to be his wife for the past seventeen years, for letting her be the mother of his children.

Her gaze shifted from her husband to her son. Arledge, at twelve, looked so much like his father. They had the same nose, the same chin, the same thoughtful expression. Arledge was easygoing like Frank. Very little ruffled his feathers.

Except for his sister.

Eliza felt a flutter of concern in her heart as she looked at Miriam.

Her daughter was as beautiful as any actress, and it wasn't just a mother's prejudice that made Eliza think so. But it wasn't her daughter's looks that caused Eliza to worry. It was Miriam's attitude. The girl was so headstrong, so willful, and so determined to become a part of the world beyond River Bluff that Eliza was afraid of what impulsive thing her daughter would do to break free. Eliza occasionally voiced her concerns to Frank, but he didn't seem to see any potential problem. So Eliza felt obliged to worry for the both of them.

She frowned as she watched Miriam. The girl sang, her expression innocent and sweet. But there was something going on in that pretty little head of hers, something not quite so innocent.

If only Eliza knew what it was.

~

Miriam lay on her belly, her arms hanging over the side of the bed as she stared down at the movie poster on the floor.

Come to Hollywood, Garbo seemed to say to her. *Come and be a star like me.*

She would have to make plans. She would have to start to work on Jacob. If she was careful and diligent, perhaps they could be on their way before August.

A knock at her door caused Miriam to gasp. She hastily rolled up the stolen poster and pushed it under her bed, then sat up. "Yes?"

The door opened, revealing her dad. "Don't you think you should be helping your mother in the kitchen?"

"She said she didn't need me."

He raised an eyebrow.

"I guess I could set the table."

"That's my girl." He held out his arm toward her and waited.

Miriam slid off her bed, swallowing an impatient sigh. She had a million things to do, and *she* had to set the dinner table. Whatever happened to resting on Sunday? She'd bet Garbo never had to set the table.

"I thought Pastor Desmond was particularly articulate this morning," her dad said as he draped his arm over her shoulders. They started down the hall. "Didn't you?"

"Mmm-hmm." She wondered what the sermon topic had been.

"It was a timely message. One we should take to heart."

She nodded, pretending agreement and understanding.

"You're young yet, pixie. Your life's been without serious storms. But they *will* come. They come to us all, sooner or later, because we live in a fallen, imperfect world. If you aren't anchored to the Rock, you'll be battered and bruised by the winds."

Sure, Dad, I know. I know. I don't need any more preaching today.

"I pray that your storms will be few and far between." He kissed the crown of her head.

"I pray the same for you, Dad." She smiled at him.

He gave her a squeeze. "Thanks."

The two of them reached the dining room just as Jacob showed up at the front door. Miriam saw him through the screen before he had a chance to knock.

"Hi, Jacob," she called. She looked at her dad. "Can Jacob join us for dinner?"

"Sure. I'll tell your mother. You set an extra place."

Miriam hurried to the door. As she pushed open the screen, she whispered, "We need to talk. Can you stay and eat? Dad said it was okay."

She knew what his answer would be. Jacob was always hungry. Maybe he really did have a hollow leg, the way her mom said.

A short while later, the Gresham family, plus Jacob McAllister, sat around the dining-room table. The pot roast, cooked with onions, potatoes, and carrots, filled the house with a delicious fragrance.

Miriam's father said, "Amen," at the close of the blessing, and Jacob's stomach growled in unison. Everybody laughed, even Jacob.

"You'd better start, son." Frank passed the vegetable platter to their guest.

"I didn't have a chance to speak to your mother at church, Jacob." Eliza took a warm roll from the basket. "How is she?"

"Fine, ma'am. Although she says her arthritis is acting up again. She's had to lay off her needlework for a week or so."

Frank asked, "Did your father hear about that beef-packing job over in Nampa?"

"Yeah, he heard." Jacob helped himself to a slice of roast beef. "He applied for it, but they hired somebody younger. He says nobody's interested in a man whose life's work's been on a farm." He glanced at Miriam, then away. "I'm gonna start work for Mr. Tucker pretty soon. I'll be clerkin' and learnin' to sell insurance."

Selling insurance? To Miriam that sounded worse than farming. Maybe the hours weren't as bad, but it had to be boring. Poor Jacob. Besides, few people had extra money to use for buying insurance policies these days, so Mooney Tucker couldn't be paying much.

Why, I'll be doing Jacob a favor, getting him out of River Bluff. Maybe I won't even have to say I'll marry him. Maybe he's looking for an excuse to get away.

~

"I can't, Miriam," Jacob said, his gaze fixed on the river, where sunlight glinted off the water's surface. "Even if I wanted to— which I don't—I couldn't leave now. I've got to start my new job soon. I've got to help my folks out. The pay might not be much, but it's *somethin'*. Maybe next year, after my dad finds work, maybe then I could go."

"You won't go even if . . ." She took hold of his hand. "Even if I promise to marry you when we get there?"

He couldn't believe she would make such an offer. He turned his head and looked straight into her eyes. "Not even then, Miriam," he answered, his voice thick with longing.

"But . . . but you *love* me, don't you?"

Jacob knew it wouldn't occur to Miriam that he could love her and not do what she wanted him to.

"Don't you love me?" she persisted.

"Yeah, I love you. You know I do." He shoved his hands into his pockets. It was the only way he could keep himself from touching her, from trying to take her into his arms and kiss her, the way he'd wanted to kiss her for too long. "You're barely fifteen, Miriam. You're too young to get married and definitely too young to strike out on your own. You're not thinking straight. The whole world is out of work. What makes you think you can get a job in Hollywood? There's plenty of pretty girls down there already. Prettier girls than you who can't get work in the movies."

Her eyes widened and her cheeks flushed.

He felt an unexpected spark of anger for the hurt she'd caused him, for making him say something that would hurt her in return. "Can you tell me that *you* want to marry *me*, Miriam? Tell me you love me. Tell me you want me to kiss you. Tell me you want to be my wife."

"Jacob, I . . . I . . . of course I love you."

He knew what she added silently: *as my best friend.* "If you loved me, you wouldn't force me to choose between your silly dream and my family."

Miriam took a step back from him. "Well then, you can go to the devil for all I care, Jacob McAllister. I'm going to California, with or without you. I thought you were my friend." Tears fell from her eyes. "I believed you when you said you loved me, but it was just a lie."

"Miriam—" He reached for her arm.

"Don't!" She jerked away. "Don't ever try to touch me again." She spun on her heel. "I hate you. I'll hate you forever." Then she ran away from him.

For the rest of his life, Jacob would feel a sharp pain in his chest whenever he stood beside that river and remembered.

CHAPTER FIVE

THE DRIVER OF THE PICKUP TRUCK AND HIS WIFE WERE SHOUTING AT each other in Spanish. Having daydreamed through her foreign language classes for the past two years, Miriam couldn't understand what they said. Besides, she had a splitting headache, a condition made worse by the squawking chickens in the crates that shared the truck bed with her. The intense heat, glaring sun, and swirling dust didn't help matters either.

And she was hungry. Miserably hungry. Why hadn't she brought along more food?

Tears welled in her eyes, and she bit her lower lip to keep them from falling. She could almost hear Jacob saying, "I told you so."

But she was determined not to think about Jacob. Not him or her father, her mother, her brother, or anybody else in River Bluff. She was pursuing her dreams. She wouldn't get stuck in a nothing little town, living a nothing little life, like the rest of them. Not Miriam Gresham. No, indeed.

Last night had been her first on the road, and though she hated to admit it, even to herself, she'd been terrified. She hadn't slept a wink. Every shadow cast by the first-quarter moon had promised to be a ravenous wolf—or something much worse!

At least she'd managed to catch a ride this morning. While sitting in the bed of this truck wasn't luxurious, it was better than the alternative. Yesterday she'd walked for miles and miles without seeing a single automobile.

She wiped the tears from her cheeks, disgusted with herself for letting them fall. She had no cause to complain. She wasn't walking at the moment, and if she was careful, she had enough money in her pocket to see her to Hollywood. By her calculations, she must be in Nevada by now. California was just one state to the west. She was almost there.

"I'm not too young," she muttered, glaring at the nearest chicken. "Shirley Temple's already a star, and she's only a little girl. For pity sakes, there's girls my age who're married and having babies." She crossed her arms over her chest and squeezed her eyes tightly shut. "I'll show Jacob. I'll show 'em all. I'll be famous. My life's gonna be one big adventure. They'll see."

The right rear wheel dropped into a rut in the road, throwing her to the side and smacking her head against the cab. The back of the truck fishtailed, slamming Miriam's shoulder against one of the crates. The driver's wife screeched, as did the majority of the chickens.

Miriam didn't try to fight the tears any longer. It was time for a good cry.

~

Small-town life fit Del Tucker like a glove. Plenty of his boyhood friends had taken off for the cities as soon as they could, but not Del. He planned to stay in River Bluff for the rest of his life.

His aunt Theodora, who'd raised Del after his folks died, hoped he would marry the Farnsdale girl. He'd lost count of the number of potlucks and church socials Aunt Theo had dragged him to this year where—by some "stroke of luck," as his aunt put it—Nancy Farnsdale was also present.

Poor Aunt Theo. Her matchmaking had gone unrewarded. As nice as Nancy was, Del had no romantic interest in her. He figured he'd know the right gal when he saw her, and he hadn't seen her yet.

Del leaned back in the desk chair and fanned himself with a wanted poster. The police station was a regular sweatbox today. Del had opened the windows on the outside chance a breeze would come up. So far, none had.

"You got that report finished for the mayor?" Wyatt Jagger, the police chief, called from the back room.

"Yes, sir. Finished it an hour ago."

Chief Jagger appeared in the doorway. He smoothed one side of his handlebar mustache between index finger and thumb, then with the opposite hand, patted his soft belly where it protruded over his silver belt buckle. "I'm going to the Bluff Diner to git me a bite to eat. Hold down the fort 'til I git back."

"Yes, sir."

Chief Jagger plucked his felt hat off the coatrack. "Won't be long."

"Take your time."

That was another thing Del liked about small-town life, he mused after the chief left the station. Police work in River Bluff was slow and easy, more about helping the good folks hereabouts than about hunting down hardened criminals destined for the state penitentiary.

Of course, there *was* the matter of the stolen movie poster. Petty theft, perhaps, but still . . .

As if summoned by his thoughts, the door opened, and Frank and Eliza Gresham—parents of Del's main suspect—entered. Immediately noting the distraught look on Eliza's face and the frown wrinkling Frank's brow, Del stopped fanning himself and straightened in his chair.

"Del," Frank began, "Miriam's run away."

Del stood. "When?"

Frank glanced at his wife, who answered, "Yesterday morning, we think. She told me she was going to the river to read where it was cool." Eliza twisted a handkerchief between her hands. "She does that a lot in the summertime. I had no reason to worry."

"Of course not." Del motioned toward a couple of chairs, but neither of the Greshams bothered to sit.

"She didn't come to the drugstore for the lunch hour like she usually does," Frank said. "We assumed she'd lost track of time. I wasn't happy about it, but—" he abruptly concluded his sentence with a shrug.

"What makes you think she ran away? Did she leave you a note?"

"No," her parents answered in unison.

Del didn't mention that occasionally tramps camped along the river when they were passing through the county. He didn't say that some of them were unsavory characters who might take advantage of a pretty young woman, were they to chance upon her.

"It was something she said to her brother," Eliza continued.

"And what was that?"

"She told him it was high time he started helping out more at the store because she wasn't going to be around to do it."

Del frowned, thinking it wasn't much to go on.

"A few of her things are gone," Frank said softly, then sighed. "There's money missing from my cash register, too." He glanced at his wife. "And . . . and we found this under her bed." He held out the stolen movie poster.

"She talks all the time about wanting to be an actress." Eliza sniffled, then pressed her head against her husband's shoulder. "We hoped she'd outgrow it."

~

The pickup was gone.

Miriam stared at the empty spot where the truck had been only a few minutes before. The farmer had stopped arguing with his wife long enough to pull into a filling station for gas. Miriam had taken the opportunity to dash into the nearby restaurant to use the rest room. When she came out, the truck and its squabbling inhabitants had disappeared.

They left me?

She glanced around, but the truck was nowhere to be seen.

I don't know where I am.

This wide spot in the road couldn't be called a town. It was only a few buildings where two state highways intersected. The gas station and restaurant were more or less one business. There was a tiny mercantile across the street and a bar kitty-corner from it.

From here, Miriam could look for miles in any direction and see nothing but flat country covered with silvery green sagebrush. Empty, desolate, lonely. A wasteland without trees, water, or civilization.

She wanted to cry, but she determinedly swallowed her tears. She wouldn't feel sorry for herself. So help her, she wouldn't.

Miriam turned toward the restaurant. She was starving. She supposed this was as good a time as any to eat. Then she would ask which was the road to California.

Surely she'd be able to find another willing farmer to help her out. One without a screaming wife and crates full of squawking chickens.

~

"Well?" Officer Tucker prompted, looking imposing in his police uniform, his brows pulled together in a demanding frown.

"I don't know where she is," Jacob answered.

"But you do know where she's going. Don't you?"

Jacob glanced at the ground. Should he lie to protect

Miriam, or should he tell the truth in order to protect her from herself?

"Her parents are worried sick, Jacob. Is she on her way to California? That's what she had in mind, isn't it?"

She already hated him because he wouldn't go with her. How much worse would it be if he told where she was going?

"Jacob." Officer Tucker's hand alighted on his shoulder. "If she's on the road alone, she could get hurt. There's all sorts wandering the highways these days. Miriam's young and she's pretty and she isn't thinking straight. Help us find her."

The man's words struck deep into Jacob's soul. "All right." He nodded, then lifted his gaze. "Yes, she was headed for California. To Hollywood. But I don't know how or when. We . . . we had a falling-out over it 'cause I wouldn't go with her."

The officer muttered to himself.

"You'll find her, won't you?"

"I'll do my best, Jacob."

~

"You might be able to hitch a ride with some of the Echeverria boys in the morning," the waitress told Miriam after hearing how she'd come to be there on foot. "I heard Zigor sayin' they were drivin' down to San Francisco. I think they're goin' tomorrow." She set the plate on the table, then turned toward the kitchen and shouted, "Mikolas, are your brothers headed for Frisco in the mornin'?"

"Yeah," came a deep voice from the back.

"They willin' to take another passenger?"

"How would I know? Why? You leaving me?"

"I just might, you keep mouthin' off to me that way." The waitress patted the back of Miriam's hand. "You eat. I'll see what I can find out 'bout gettin' you a ride outta here."

"Thanks," Miriam whispered.

"Don't worry," the woman added with a kindly smile. "There's a cot in the back room. You can sleep there tonight. Keep you away from the rattlers."

Miriam swallowed a lump in her throat. She was hungry and dirty, tired and scared. She didn't know whether to be relieved by this woman's offer of help or wish someone would send her packing for home.

~

Eliza came out of the kitchen, drying her hands on a dish towel. She stopped when she saw her husband. He was sitting in his favorite chair, leaning forward, his elbows resting on his thighs, the *Anna Karenina* poster held between his hands. His expression revealed a tortured heart.

"Del will find her," she said as she approached him.

Frank glanced up. There were tears in his eyes. She couldn't remember the last time she'd seen him cry. Was it the night Arledge was born?

"She did something foolish, but she's got a good head on her shoulders, too." Eliza sat on the arm of Frank's chair. "She'll be okay."

"I should have seen this coming. You tried to warn me, but I wouldn't listen."

She wanted to tell him it wasn't his fault, that he'd been a good father to their children, but he was all too ready to cast recriminations at himself at the moment. Later, after Miriam was home, Frank would see . . .

The breath caught in her throat, a strangled sound of fear. What if Miriam never came home? She pressed a fist to her mouth, fighting sudden panic.

Frank tossed the poster aside, then drew Eliza from the arm

of the chair and onto his lap. He held her close, his face pressed into her hair.

"Father in heaven, keep our little girl safe," he whispered. "Del doesn't know where she is, but You do. Help him find her. Put Your angels around and about her. We're asking for Your mercy and grace to be shed upon her and this situation, in the name of Jesus." His arms tightened around Eliza. "Please, Father God, hear my heart's cry. Protect our little girl. Keep her safe and bring her home to us. Amen."

~

There was no window in the storeroom at the back of the restaurant. Actually, it was little more than a broom closet.

Somewhere around midnight, Miriam was forced to open the door or suffocate. Afterward, she returned to the cot and lay down, staring upward in the darkness. Tears slipped from her eyes and slid across her temples and into her hair. She didn't bother to wipe them away. They were falling too fast. Her throat hurt and so did her chest.

Her folks would know what she'd done by now. They would know she'd run away from home. They would know she took money from the cash register. They'd be disappointed in her.

Would they guess where she was headed? If they didn't, she supposed Jacob would tell them. The snitch.

I hate you. I'll hate you forever.

No, she didn't hate Jacob. Not really. He could make her madder than all get-out, but she couldn't hate him. He couldn't help being the way he was, any more than she could help being the way she was.

She heard the sound of a squeaking door hinge, then footsteps on the wooden floor outside. A man's footsteps, not a woman's. Coming closer.

Miriam sat up on the cot and turned toward the open door to the storeroom. Should she try to close it? There was a lock. If she moved quickly, she might—

A light came on in the kitchen. There was a moment of silence, then the approaching footsteps again. Fear squeezed the air from her lungs. Suddenly, he was there, framed in the doorway, a large black silhouette—sinister, threatening.

What do you want? Panic silenced her question before it could claw its way from her throat.

"Miriam Gresham—"

Even in her terrified state, she recognized Officer Tucker's voice.

"You're under arrest."

JULIANNA

Summer 2001

CHAPTER SIX

I SUCKED IN A TINY GASP. "HE *ARRESTED* HER?"

"Yup," the old man said with a chuckle. "Del trussed Miriam up and hauled her back to River Bluff, giving her a piece of his mind the whole way." He shook his head. "She wouldn't admit it at first, not for years actually, but she was mighty glad to see him. Later on, she figured that all-night-long lecture was worth being rescued from her own stupidity."

"Did she ever make it to Hollywood?"

"No, she never did."

"That's too bad. She wanted it so much."

I considered the dreams I used to have for my future. In high school, I wanted a career in journalism. I planned to go to the university for four years. After that, I imagined I would travel the world, on assignment for one of the country's major newspapers.

Only before any of that happened, I met Leland and fell in love. I delayed starting college for a year so we could marry. It seemed worth it at the time. But an unexpected pregnancy put an end to my lofty plans, once and for all.

"Guess you didn't know Miriam very well," the old man said, interrupting my thoughts.

"No. I didn't know her at all. I . . . I came for the preview, and when I saw the box and read what was written on the top, my curiosity got the better of me and I . . ." I let my babbling explanation fade into silence, feeling guilty for opening this box of memories.

"Miriam would've wanted you to look. She—"

The sitting-room door opened, interrupting him and drawing our gazes.

A woman who looked to be in her mid-sixties was the first to enter. Pleasantly plump with thinning light brown hair, she grinned broadly when she saw us. "Jacob!" she exclaimed. "You're early!"

Miriam's Jacob? I should have guessed.

Jacob stood. "Hello, Sally." He looked beyond. "Sean. Christy. Glad you're here."

Sean was a handsome man, about my age, with graying hair near his temples. I had the feeling I should know him, but I couldn't think from where.

Christy was young enough to be Sean's daughter, although I saw no family resemblance. Petite with pixie-short, spiky brown hair, she wore bright yellow shorts and a white tank top.

"Come in and sit down." Jacob motioned toward the chairs. "I was telling—" He stopped abruptly, eyebrows raised as he looked at me. "Sorry. Guess I didn't get your name."

"Julianna Crosby," I answered, certain I should leave these friends to their memories. I opened my mouth to make my excuses, but I was too late.

"It's nice to meet you, Julianna." Sean offered a warm smile, and again I thought I should know him.

As he sank onto his chair, Jacob continued, "I was telling Julianna about Miriam and the things in her life box."

The others smiled and nodded as if they shared a secret. The next thing I knew, we were all seated around that small coffee table.

"I remember thinking," Christy said, "the first time I saw these things, what a strange collection of junk it was."

My curiosity took over. I glanced at Jacob and asked, "Why did she pick these particular things?"

"Guess it's obvious it wasn't for their monetary value." He winked at me. "No, Miriam chose 'em for personal reasons. Things she learned. Precious memories." He lifted the faded service cap from the box, then let it drape through the fingers of his right hand. "Some of the lessons she learned came hard. Not just for her, but for the whole country."

"Was that cap yours?" I asked softly.

"No, it belonged to her husband, Del."

"Del?" My surprised gaze moved from Jacob to the others and back again. "The *cop?*"

Jacob chuckled. "Yup."

"How did *that* happen?"

"She grew up." He shrugged, then looked at the cap again. "Once she did, Del fell for her hard, and he wasn't about to let her get away, even though she was livin' here in Boise at the time. He was as dogged in his courtship of her as he was in pursuit of any criminal. Miriam never had a chance."

"But why did she choose him and not you?" I regretted the question the instant it was out of my mouth.

Jacob didn't seem to mind. "Plenty of reasons, I suppose. For one thing, I think she always saw me more as a brother and couldn't get past that. But mostly, it was 'cause those two were just plain meant to be together." He stroked the cap. "'Course I didn't realize it back then."

MIRIAM

SPRING 1944

CHAPTER SEVEN

Miriam Tucker locked the front door of the Main Street Pharmacy, then slipped the key into her pocketbook before starting down the sidewalk toward home.

Her *parents'* home, she amended, feeling a sting of resentment. Nearly twenty-three, married, and still in River Bluff, living with her mother while running her father's drugstore.

She pressed her lips together and quickened her footsteps.

Main Street was deserted as dusk settled over River Bluff. Not a single automobile in sight. There was *rarely* a car in sight these days. The war and gas rationing had seen to that. What gasoline there was in River Bluff was For Farmers Only, as the sign on the Texaco pump said.

Essential use.

Miriam was sick to death of phrases like that. She was sick to death of never being able to do anything fun or go anywhere exciting. She was sick of going bare-legged in summer and winter because she couldn't buy hosiery. She was sick of the sameness of every day. She was sick of living in a town where the only males were schoolboys and old men. She was sick of scrap drives and fat collection drives and rubber drives and every other kind of drive. She was sick of food rationing, of not being able to have something particular to eat because the family had no ration coupon for it. She was sick of using things up, wearing things out, making things do, or doing without.

"Oh, Miriam! Miriam Tucker, *wait!*"

She cringed at the sound of Grace Finch's voice, but she stopped and turned.

Holding on to her ridiculous-looking hat, Grace hurried across the street, her face turning red from the exertion. "How are you, dear?"

"Fine, Mrs. Finch. And you?"

"Fair to middlin'. My back's been bothering me a lot lately, but I can't complain."

But you will, won't you?

"Dr. Carson says there just isn't anything more he can do for me. It's age, he says, and he can't stop that. He doesn't understand how much it pains me to sit and play the organ."

And you don't know how much it pains me to listen to you play.

"Any news?" Grace asked, not needing to explain her question. Everybody understood those words these days.

"We had a letter from my dad yesterday." Miriam turned and started walking with long, determined strides.

Grace fell in beside her. "Is Frank still in Portland?"

"Yes."

"It must be awful for him, living and working so far from home. Heaven knows what sort of housing he's found. I understand it's the same across the country. Men living in tar-paper shacks, and heaven forbid, women too. It's positively shameful the way so many wives and mothers are working in those war plants when their place is at home. My goodness, the sacrifices we've had to make in the war effort."

Miriam said nothing.

"Of course, it's far worse for our boys at the front, isn't it? You must be grateful your husband is stateside. I'm sure the army's glad to have him training their recruits. Del was always good with the young people of this town." Grace waved at Gard Holbright as he left the bank, then turned her attention once more to Miriam. "Where did you say Del was stationed?"

"I didn't say," Miriam replied tersely. "Loose lips sink ships."

Grace didn't have the good sense to know she'd been insulted. Instead, she laughed. "You're so right, my dear." She patted Miriam's arm. "Well, here's my corner. Give my best to your mother. I'll catch up on news about Arledge next time I see her." She scurried down the street, once again holding on to her hat with one hand, as if she were moving so fast she feared it would blow off her head.

Anger and frustration surged in Miriam's heart.

Fat old busybody.

She turned her face heavenward and demanded, "Why did You do this to me? It isn't fair." Then she continued toward home.

But even in a foul mood, she recognized that God hadn't created a world war just to cause trouble for Miriam Tucker, even if it did feel that way.

She sighed as her thoughts drifted backward in time. It helped to search out the good memories, to remind herself that there had been better times, that her life hadn't always been like this, that her husband and her brother hadn't always been in the military, that her father hadn't always lived five hundred miles from home, that she hadn't always been stuck in River Bluff, working at the drugstore and living with her mother.

No, it hadn't always been like this. She remembered . . .

The summer she graduated from high school, Miriam moved to Boise. She found employment as a switchboard operator for the state government and rented a small apartment with two other young women. Away from her parents' watchful eyes, she stopped going to church, usually because she was dancing until all hours on Saturday nights and was too tired on Sunday mornings to get out of bed before noon.

Oh, the fun she had! She particularly enjoyed the men who

came calling, trying to win her affections. Like a cat turned loose in a creamery, Miriam lapped up their adoration, accepting their gifts and flowers as if they were her due.

She received three proposals of marriage before the end of her first year in the capital city. Not that she seriously considered accepting any of them. Not for a moment.

And then, one Saturday afternoon in the fall of 1940, Del Tucker appeared on her front porch. To this day she wasn't certain when he had changed from being the stern older officer of the law into the handsome suitor who was destined to steal her heart. She seemed to forget it was Del who'd arrested her and taken her back to River Bluff, humiliated and chagrined only a few years earlier.

Their courtship—and later, their engagement—was slow and old-fashioned. Del drove to Boise on his days off, and Miriam visited River Bluff on the weekends, ostensibly to see her parents, but everyone in town knew it was so she and Del could spend more time together. Every moment they were apart was torturous for Miriam.

She could still recall the joy she felt when Del told her his application to the Boise Police Department had been accepted. His new job was to start right after the new year, in January 1942.

Miriam and Del were married on November 15, three weeks and a day before Pearl Harbor. Blissfully unaware of what the future had in store, they settled into an apartment in Boise, certain that love was all they needed to be happy forever.

But Del never started with the Boise police force. Instead, he enlisted in the United States Army and was gone from Idaho— and from his wife's side—before they were married four months.

Miriam stopped when she reached the sidewalk that led to the Gresham front door. Through a blur of unwelcome tears, she stared at the house while wishing she could hit something.

Anything! Better yet, she'd like to take a sock at a few hard-headed males. She'd like to punch every one of them smack-dab on their stubborn, albeit patriotic, chins.

She would have started with Del. Why had he felt compelled to enlist? Why couldn't he have waited until he was drafted? Who knew how many more months they would have had together? Maybe, since he was a police officer, he wouldn't have been drafted at all.

Then there was her dad. Why had he taken that defense plant job in Portland? He was forty-eight, for pity's sake. He could have stayed home and seen to his own store, instead of relying on Miriam to return to River Bluff and mind it for him. If not for the store, she could have joined Del in California, like other army wives.

And she'd like to blacken *both* of Arledge's eyes. The idiot had enlisted the day he turned eighteen, with scarcely a thought for how their mother would feel about her baby going to war. He had already spent a year on the opposite side of the Atlantic, although his letters home never gave an exact location.

Jacob McAllister was on her list of troublesome males, too. He was piloting planes somewhere in the Pacific. He deserved an extra hard thump on the head, as far as she was concerned. She'd have thought at least *he*—of all people!—would've considered *her* feelings before rushing off to get himself shot or maimed or . . . or killed.

She swallowed the sob that rose in her throat and swept the fallen tears from her cheeks.

In defeat, she admitted she wasn't angry with any of them. Not with Del, her father, her brother, or Jacob. She wasn't angry; she was afraid. Afraid that she, like so many women across the country, might lose someone she loved.

Grace Finch was right. Miriam should be grateful that Del was training recruits at a military camp in the States instead of serving overseas. And she was. As long as Del was stateside—even if she couldn't be with him—she needn't fear for his safety the way she did for Arledge's and Jacob's. She might miss him horribly, but at least he was safe. He wrote twice a week and called home once a month.

Yes, she had much to be grateful for. The next time she felt sorry for herself and cursed the inconveniences of war, she would try to remember that.

~

Del stared out the living-room window, captivated by the first sight of his wife in more than two years. She'd cut her hair to just above her shoulders. Golden curls framed her face. He could only imagine the effort she went to each morning to accomplish that look. She was thinner than he remembered, but she always had been a slight thing.

He smiled, remembering how he'd thought the teenage Miriam was nothing but trouble and would never be anything else. That night he found her in Nevada, he'd told her she should be locked in her room and the key thrown away. He'd meant it, too.

Just went to prove that God had a fine sense of humor.

It had been a shock to Del's sense of order and justice that day, four years before, when he saw Miriam—who seemed to have become a woman overnight—and realized his attraction to the former juvenile delinquent. It had taken another six months to talk himself into driving to Boise and calling on her.

It still surprised him that he'd won her heart, that she'd agreed to marry him. She could have had any guy she wanted. There'd certainly been plenty of them hanging around in Boise. Guys closer to her own age, too. Why on earth she'd given Del a second look, he still hadn't figured out.

But she'd done more than give him a second look. She'd given him her heart.

Unable to wait another instant, he strode to the front door, yanked it open, and stepped onto the porch. Miriam gazed at him for a moment, disbelief written across her pretty face. Then, as if suddenly realizing he wasn't a figment of her imagination, she dropped her handbag and raced toward him.

"Del! Del, it's you!" She threw herself into his arms. "It's really you!"

He kissed her mouth. He kissed her cheeks. He kissed her temples. He kissed the tip of her nose.

"Oh, Del. You're home! You're home. You're really here! Really and truly here."

"Really and truly." He kept right on kissing her, tasting the salt of her tears, holding her close, never wanting to let go.

Eventually he would have to. Eventually he would have to tell her that he was shipping out. But he didn't want to think about that now. Later, but not now.

"Why didn't you tell me you were coming?" she whispered when their lips finally parted and they came up for air.

"I didn't know until a few days ago. I wanted to surprise you."

"Oh, you did. You really did." She cupped his face between the palms of her hands while staring into his eyes. "I've missed you so much. I can't believe you're here. How long can you stay?"

He kissed her again before answering. "A week."

"Only a week? But Del—"

"That's all the United States Army can spare me." He gave her a cocky grin, hoping to tease away her disappointment. "I'm indispensable. Haven't you heard?"

"I *hate* the army."

Del placed an index finger over her lips. "Don't say that, Miriam."

She drew back from him, a frown creasing her forehead. "I can't help it. I want you with me."

"Soon," he said softly. "I think it'll be over soon."

"Really?"

He nodded, then drew her back into his embrace. *Please, God, let it be over soon.*

CHAPTER EIGHT

MIRIAM DIPPED HER TOES INTO THE ICY COLD WATER, THEN QUICKLY drew them out, thankful for the warmth of the spring sunshine upon her back.

"How can you bear to be out there?" she called. "It's freezing."

Standing in the middle of the river, his legs encased in hip waders, Del cast his line before answering. "I'm numb. Can't feel a thing." He grinned.

Miriam's breath caught in her throat. Love and dread caused a fluttering in her stomach. How would she bear it when he left her again? Already two days of his leave had whisked by. In another five . . .

"*Wahoo!*"

At the excited cry, Miriam focused her gaze and watched as Del reeled in the line, a large trout at the opposite end making a valiant struggle to escape the hook in its mouth.

"It's fish for supper," her husband shouted.

If not for the war, how many times might they have spent a day like this? If not for the war . . .

The dread returned, heavier this time, like a lead weight upon her heart.

Del scooped the trout into his net, then held it above his head in a gesture of triumph.

Miriam made herself smile. She didn't want her fear to spoil the moment.

With careful steps, Del moved through the turbulent water toward the bank, still grinning, eyes sparkling, water glittering on his face and bare arms. "No ration coupon needed for this big fella. I'll clean him if you'll cook him."

"It's a deal." She stood. "Now we'd better get you home and into something dry before you catch your death." The instant she said it, she wished she hadn't. The words seemed ominous, dangerous.

"A little cold water never hurt anybody."

That isn't true. People drown. People catch pneumonia. Sometimes cold water hurts people. Miriam felt strangled by her own panic.

"Honey?" Del wasn't smiling anymore. He set aside his pole and net before stepping close and gathering her into his arms. "What's wrong?"

"I don't want you to go back, Del. Not without me. I can't bear it. Can't I go with you? I could live in a town near the camp." Tears filled her eyes, then spilled down her cheeks. "We could see each other every day. Mother could manage the store during the summer months at least. She could do it while school's out. Then maybe Dad would come home if I weren't here in his place. Oh, Del, I—" she stopped abruptly, choking on a sob.

"Shh." He brushed his lips across her forehead. "Don't cry, Miriam. Please."

She swallowed hard, but it didn't stop the tears.

"You can't go with me, baby," he whispered.

"Why not? Why not?"

He drew a deep breath as he pulled her tight against him, pressing her cheek against his chest. And even before he spoke, she knew what he was going to say.

"Because I'm shipping out."

If not for his arms around her, she would have crumpled. "But they . . . but they need you to . . . to train soldiers."

"They *did* need me to train. Now they need me to fight."

"No." She drew her head back, looked up to meet his gaze. "No, I won't let you go."

His smile was sad, tender. "I don't have any choice. Neither do you."

Tears blurred her vision, and a lump in her throat made it momentarily impossible to speak.

"We have to trust God to see us through this."

"That's what everybody says."

Del caressed the side of her face. "And do you?"

"Do I what?"

"Do you trust God?" His dark gaze searched hers.

She thought of the hours her mother had spent in prayer since the war began and especially since those closest to her had gone to serve their country.

Had those prayers been answered?

Had *anybody's* prayers been answered?

"Do you trust Him, Miriam?"

Her voice filled with anguish and frustration. "I don't know."

She stepped back, out of his embrace, crossing her arms over her chest as if to ward him off. But Del didn't attempt to draw her close again. He simply stared at her, his eyes sad, his thoughts hidden.

Miriam felt utterly alone.

~

There was so much Del wanted to say to his wife, yet he couldn't find the words. Maybe because this faith in God was new to him. And that seemed strange, too. After all, he'd been raised in the church. He'd spent his life singing hymns of worship and listening to his aunt and uncle praying and reading the Bible. He couldn't recall a time when he hadn't believed that

Jesus was the Son of God, but it had been a distant belief, not personal.

Then something had happened to Del while he was in California, training young recruits to go off to war. He couldn't say what it was for certain. Just seemed one day he woke up and knew that he was different, that his faith was different. Suddenly, he knew that he knew that Jesus was with him. He knew Jesus loved him and had him in mind when He went to the cross. That morning, Jesus had become not only his Savior but his Lord, and Del believed that Jesus would see him through whatever came in the days, weeks, and months ahead.

He wanted Miriam to know it, too.

"Let's go home, Del," she said softly, interrupting his thoughts.

"Honey, I—"

She raised a hand to stop him. "Let's not talk anymore. Not now."

"But—"

"Please, Del."

Maybe he should have tried harder to say what was in his heart, but time and distance had made strangers of them. Loving, intimate strangers, yes, but strangers all the same. Funny, that he hadn't realized it before.

Lord, I've forgotten how to talk to her. I'm so used to barking orders, I've forgotten how to just plain talk to my wife about the things that matter most.

Miriam picked up the fishing pole. "Are you coming?" Her words were clipped, her voice strained.

"Yeah, I'm coming."

She took off before he could gather the rest of his gear and the trout he'd caught for their supper. He decided it was better to give her time to adjust to the news. He supposed she had a right to be mad. He should have told her about his orders when he first arrived in River Bluff, but he'd wanted to be with her first, without thoughts of the war intruding. He'd wanted to hold her and kiss her and love her with every fiber of his being.

What if something happens to me, and I can't take care of her?

Taking care of Miriam was what Del most wanted to do.

God, I love her. Let me come back. Let me come back a whole man so I can be the kind of husband she needs.

Del knew something big was coming in the European theater. Not that he'd been told anything officially, but he'd been in the military long enough to recognize certain signs. The Allies were gathering for a major assault. Even the Germans had to know that much.

He wondered if Miriam would understand that he was relieved to be going overseas at last, that he needed to do something more than train other men to shoot guns and follow orders, that he needed to feel he was actively protecting the country he loved. But he knew the answer was no—she wouldn't understand.

Maybe I don't understand it myself.

~

It was one of those perfect spring days. The sky was a cloudless, powder blue, the breeze sweet and fresh. The leaves on the trees that lined Church Street were glorious shades of green, from deepest emerald to palest lime. Tulips and daffodils dipped their colorful heads to each and every passerby.

But Eliza Gresham scarcely noticed the world around her as she walked home. It had been a difficult day for everyone at River Bluff Elementary, for the word had come that eight-year-old Sally Pritchett's brother was dead, killed in action in the Pacific.

Eliza didn't know the Pritchetts well. The family lived on a farm a good fifteen miles from town, and they didn't attend the same church as the Greshams. Still, she didn't need to know them to understand how much they were suffering.

Father God, how many more must be lost before this war is over? How long will You allow these atrocities to continue?

She clutched her pocketbook close to her breast.

Don't let it be me, Lord. I've no right to ask, but I'm asking anyway. Don't let it be me who gets one of those telegrams.

As she turned the corner onto Elm, she purposely turned her thoughts in another direction as well—to her daughter and Del.

Miriam had closed the drugstore for the past two days so she could spend the time with Del. While Frank might not have approved, Eliza thought it a wise decision. The young couple needed time together. Eliza was certain this leave meant Del's orders had changed, although he hadn't said so to her.

"Poor Miriam."

Those two words replayed in her mind and heart as she followed the sidewalk to the front door of her home. But her worries were forgotten the instant she saw the letters in the mailbox—one from Frank and another from Arledge.

She sank onto the top step of the porch and opened the letter from her husband first.

Dearest Eliza,

I didn't receive a letter from you today. I hadn't realized how much I'd been hoping for one until I saw it wasn't there. I'm so hungry for word from home. They say no news is good news, but I'm not convinced that's true.

The rains continue, and I feel depression settling over me like one of these weeping gray clouds. When I return to Idaho, I swear I won't complain again about the heat of summer or the dry climate.

Morale at the plant is low. Several men recently lost loved ones— sons and brothers. It gets where I don't want to meet anybody's eyes or become anybody's friend because I'm afraid of what I might have to go through with them. Then I'm ashamed of myself. Hasn't God blessed us? Hasn't He promised to go with us through all the storms of life? He said He would never leave or forsake us. I can take Him at His word. I wonder how anybody makes it through times like this without faith in God. I don't know how I would.

Mrs. Ingles has loaned me her grandson's bicycle, which has made getting around a lot easier. I can get back and forth between the plant and the boardinghouse much faster now that I don't take the plant bus. Not that it's much fun to ride in the rain. It isn't. But it seems I'm wet all the time anyway, so I guess it doesn't matter.

I got a letter from Jacob McAllister last week. He didn't say much, except that he loves flying. He made it sound like a great adventure, but I know better. It's war.

You know what I think about most? You. Lying here in my lumpy bed in this cold, damp attic room in this gray, bleak city, I remember the sunshine on your hair and the way you tip your face upward when you laugh and the lovely sparkle in your eyes. I think of how quick you are to reach out to someone in need, the way you give your heart away to others. Like it was only yesterday, I remember the day you told me you were expecting Miriam. Of course, we didn't know it was Miriam. We just knew it was the baby we both wanted.

I love you, Eliza. Tell Miriam I send her my love as well. I miss you both.
Always,
Frank

"I remember, too, darling," Eliza whispered as she carefully refolded the letter, at the same time blinking back tears. "I remember everything. I miss you so much." She kissed the envelope. Silly, perhaps, but she hoped Frank would feel it across the miles.

She closed her eyes for a moment and said a quick prayer for her husband. Then she lifted the second envelope and broke the seal.

Dear Mom,

I hope this letter finds you and Miriam well. It's been awhile since I've had a chance to write, and our mail hasn't been coming through very regular either, so I've got no idea what's happening at home.

I spent a few days last month in a military hospital. Nothing serious, so no cause for alarm. Seems this climate where we've been doesn't suit me much. I'm back with my unit now, and it looks like we'll be sent to a different front real soon. Can't tell you where, even if the censors would let me, which they won't. Guess it's going to be a surprise to us all.

I know you worry lots about me, but I got to tell you that I'm getting used to Uncle Sam's Army. Maybe when this war's over, I'll finish my education and then make this my career. If I could be an officer, it wouldn't be half bad.

Time for chow. I'll write again soon as I can.
Your loving son,
Arledge

~

When Miriam saw her mother sitting on the front step, staring at a piece of paper in her hands, she immediately thought the worst. Heart in her throat, she ran the rest of the way to her.

"Mother?"

Eliza looked up. "We've got letters from your dad and Arledge." She waved the paper in the air.

Miriam came to a halt. "Everything's okay?"

"Yes." Her mother smiled. "They're both fine."

Miriam sighed. "Thank goodness."

"Thank God," Eliza replied. Then, looking beyond Miriam, she asked, "Where's Del?"

"He's coming. At least I think he is. I left him at the river."

Her mother gave her a piercing look. "Something wrong?"

Even as Miriam shook her head, she said, "We had a fight."

"Want to tell me about it?"

This time she shook her head and meant it. She wouldn't dream of telling her mother that she wasn't sure she trusted God. Eliza Gresham would be crushed by such a confession coming from her daughter.

But why *should* Miriam trust the Almighty? Too many people were dead. Too many were suffering. Too many horrible things were happening in the world. How could anyone believe God loved them, that He cared what they were doing?

What if there isn't a God at all?

Her heart thudded.

"Miriam, dear . . ." Eliza laid a hand on her daughter's arm. "Pray about it."

For a moment, she wondered if her mother had read her mind.

"Don't let the sun go down on your anger," Eliza continued. "Obeying that simple principle will keep your marriage strong. No matter what's happened during the day, ask forgiveness and forgive him. Then you can go to sleep in peace."

"Peace." Miriam sank onto the step beside her mother. "Do you think we'll ever have peace again? Real peace, I mean."

"Of course."

Miriam stared at her hands, folded in her lap. "Del's being sent overseas."

"Oh, sweetie. I'm sorry." Her mother draped an arm around Miriam's shoulders. "Europe or the Pacific?"

She tried to recall, then had to confess, "I don't know. I didn't let him tell me."

Eliza gave her a squeeze.

"I know it isn't his fault, Mother. He has to go where the army sends him. I just feel so . . . so helpless."

"It's hard to be separated from the one you love. Especially when you're young and newly married." Eliza's gaze lowered to the letters in her lap. With a sigh, she added, "Time passes slowly when all you live for is someone's return. Sometimes I feel sorry for myself. The house is empty without your father in it, and the bed seems so big and cold at night. I don't like sleeping alone. I hate being the one left behind. And then I remember what the men are going through, all that they're sacrificing, and I'm ashamed of my selfishness. I'm ashamed of my lack of faith."

"That doesn't sound like you."

Softly, Eliza replied, "There are secrets in every woman's heart, my dear. Even your mother's."

CHAPTER NINE

MIRIAM LAY IN THE BED BESIDE DEL, WATCHING AS EARLY MORNING sunlight chased shadows of night across the ceiling.

Two days. Only two days of his leave left.

Del groaned softly in his sleep. Miriam turned her head on the pillow so she could look at him.

I don't want him to go.

She adored his disheveled appearance, his hair turned every which way, his jaw darkened by stubble. She loved the way he'd held her last night, the way he'd whispered sweet words in her ear, the tenderness in his strong hands, and the passion of his kisses.

Her mother's words of three days ago echoed in her memory: *"The house is empty without your father in it, and the bed seems so big and cold at night. I don't like sleeping alone."*

Miriam knew exactly what her mother meant. She didn't like sleeping alone either. She wanted to wake up beside Del every morning. It seemed unfair that she couldn't.

"There are secrets in every woman's heart, my dear."

Secrets. Feelings too deep. Memories too precious. She felt a special kinship with her mother, no longer simply as parent and child but as part of a sisterhood of women—women who were left behind to worry and wonder.

Del's eyelids fluttered open, and he met Miriam's gaze with a sleepy one of his own. Then he gave her a slow smile. "Morning," he said, his voice deep and husky. He reached for her and drew her close against his side. "Sleep good?"

"Mmm."

"Me, too."

She kissed his shoulder before laying her head against it.

"Penny for your thoughts."

"Nothing in particular," she whispered.

"And everything in general?"

She smiled. "I suppose."

Morning light continued to invade the bedroom, sliding down the wall opposite the window, gilding the purple-flowered wallpaper.

"Miriam, I think we need to discuss some things. Monday will be here before we—"

"I don't want to talk about your leaving."

He shifted, drawing slightly away before rolling onto his side. "We can't pretend it isn't coming."

"I *want* to pretend." She squeezed her eyes closed. "Pretending suits me just fine."

"Miriam . . ."

"Please, Del."

"No, honey. That worked a few days ago. But we can't ignore the inevitable forever."

She opened her eyes again, fighting tears. "Why not?"

"Because we both know there's a chance I might not come back."

"Don't say such a thing. It's bad luck."

His smile was full of patience. "I don't believe in luck. I believe in God."

"So do I, but—"

He placed his index finger over her lips. "Hear me out."

She didn't want to, but neither could she deny him his request. Not when he would soon go away. Not when she knew he might never return, that she might lose him forever, just as he'd said.

"It's not hard to believe in God, Miriam. Most people only have to look at nature and all He's created to believe there's a God. Most Americans go to church and believe Jesus lived, once upon a time. But they don't *know* Him. They don't grasp the reality that He died for them, then rose from the dead and is *still* alive. He wants to walk with each and every one of us all the days of our lives. He wants to love us with an everlasting love."

Miriam heard the urgency in his voice and saw it in his eyes. She wished she understood why it was there. How he could talk so personally about God, as if somehow he knew Him.

Del continued, more softly now. "I didn't understand it myself. I went to church, listened to the preacher, and tried to live right, tried to follow the Ten Commandments. But I didn't understand the reality of the Christian message. Then one day, down there in California, I did. I met Him, and that moment changed my life. It changed me. *He* changed me."

"Who?"

"Jesus."

"Oh."

Del caressed the side of her face with his fingertips. "I want you to know Him, too. To know Him in your heart."

Anger welled suddenly. She rolled away and sat up, lowering her feet over the side of the bed. "If He loves you so much, why's He sending you away, maybe to be killed?"

"I don't know why, but I know He'll go with me." His hand alighted on her shoulder. She felt the bed shift and knew he was sitting up behind her. "Miriam, if you were to have a baby, I'd want—"

She twisted to look at him. *"What?"*

Her expression obviously amused him, for he grinned. "It's possible. We haven't done anything to prevent it, you know."

"Of course, I know." Heat rose in her cheeks.

His smile faded. "If we have a child as a result of this leave and I don't come back from the war, I want him to know that his father loved God and wasn't afraid of dying." He kissed her cheek. "If that happens, will you tell him?" He searched her eyes earnestly.

She couldn't stay angry. Not when her heart was breaking. "I'll tell him."

~

The train depot in Boise hummed with activity. Most of the men—like Del—were in uniform. Most of the women—like Miriam—were fighting tears.

She'd never hated anything as much as she hated the sight of that train pulling into the station. The moment of Del's departure had arrived, the weeklong leave disappearing like vapor above a kettle. So short a time. So many words left unspoken. So many fears still unconquered. So many dreams yet unfulfilled.

Wordlessly, communicating only with their eyes, they walked out of the depot to the platform, Miriam clinging to Del's arm. Steam *shoosh*ed from beneath the yellow engine. The sun, hotter than normal for May, beat upon their heads. Hasty farewells and lovers' kisses were exchanged all around them.

"Miriam, try not to be afraid."

"I can't help it."

He kissed her forehead, then whispered, "Remember, God tells us not to fear because He's with us."

She didn't want to talk about God. She didn't want to be preached at. She wanted her husband at home. She wanted to see him off to work every morning and see him come home to her every night. She wanted him to be safe. If God loved her so much, then why was He taking Del away?

"Miriam?" He brushed the tears from her cheeks with his lips. "It's going to be all right."

She nodded but couldn't speak over the lump in her throat.

"I'll write as often as I can, but don't worry if letters don't come regularly. It'll just be because the mails are held up by the army."

She swallowed hard. "I'll send V-mails often, and I'll write long letters, too."

"I'll think about you all the time. I'll pray for you every night."

"Me, too."

"Send along word about your parents and Arledge."

"I will. I promise."

"When I get home, I'll buy you a dozen pairs of silk stockings."

She sniffed, then offered a pitiful smile. "I'll cook you steaks every night for supper."

At the far end of the platform, a man shouted, "All aboard!"

Miriam threw her arms around Del's neck. "Look out for yourself. Please be careful."

"Always."

"Oh, Del, I'm sorry I wasn't . . . I'm sorry I didn't . . . I—"

"It's okay, baby. It's okay. I love you."

"All aboard!"

"Del—"

"I've gotta go." He kissed her, hungrily but too quickly.

"Del," she sobbed as he withdrew from her. "Oh, Del."

"I love you, Miriam. Just remember that. I love you."

"I love you, too."

"Take care of yourself."

"I will."

"Be good to your mom."

"I will."

He placed his foot on the first step of the railcar. "I'll be home as soon as I can."

"I'll be waiting right here."

"I love you."

"Me, too." She hugged herself, no longer able to see him through the blur of tears. She blinked hard, but by the time her vision cleared, he'd disappeared inside. Desperation welling in her chest, she searched every window for a glimpse of him.

Another burst of steam shot from beneath the engine. The train jerked forward, then paused, as if holding its breath.

"Please, God. Let me find him. Please."

Another groan, another jerk, another *shoosh* and cloud of steam.

Then he was there, leaning out of a window. "I love you, Miriam," he called to her.

"I love you, Del," she shouted back, hurrying toward him, her arm outstretched, wanting to touch him, needing to hold on, if only for a second longer.

But she couldn't get to him in time. The next turn of the iron wheels carried Del's car beyond the end of the platform. He called something to her, but she couldn't understand over the noise of the train and the shouts of departing soldiers, sailors, and airmen and their bereft wives, mothers, and sweethearts.

Something inside Miriam seemed to shrivel as she watched the train pull out of the station. And if Del died, she swore she would hate God forever.

CHAPTER TEN

THE MORNING MIRIAM DISCOVERED SHE WASN'T PREGNANT, SHE stood in the shower and wept.

And wept.

And wept.

She wept until her tears were spent, the stream turned cold, and she stood shivering beneath the spray. Finally, teeth chattering, she turned off the water, then dried herself with a towel. A few moments later, she was in front of the bathroom mirror, staring at her reflection. She placed one hand over her flat abdomen.

"What would it be like to have his baby?" she whispered. "Del's son."

If he doesn't come back, you'll never know.

Her throat ached at the thought.

A rap on the door preceded her mother's voice. "Miriam, are you all right, dear? You've been in there a long time."

"I'm fine." She sounded almost normal. "Sorry for hogging the bathroom. I'll be out shortly."

"You needn't rush. I'm leaving for school. I've left your breakfast on the stove."

"Thanks."

"Oh, would you mail a letter to your father on your way to the drugstore? It's on the kitchen table next to my Bible."

"Okay."

There was a pause; then her mother said, "Have a good day, darling."

"Thanks." Miriam felt her throat constricting and was surprised to find her vision blurred by tears again. "You, too."

Somehow she knew her mother hesitated a moment more in the hallway before turning and walking away.

"Oh, Mama," she whispered when she heard the front door close. "I didn't know I wanted a baby. How can it hurt so bad when I didn't even know?"

She drew a shaky breath, then let it out slowly before tossing the bath towel aside and beginning to dress. It didn't take long to get ready for work. She didn't care what she looked like. What did it matter with Del so far away?

With a heavy heart, she left the bathroom and went to the kitchen. After a quick glimpse at the cooked oatmeal, she carried the pan to the garbage pail and dumped the cereal into it. She couldn't think about eating. Not feeling the way she did.

Why couldn't Del and I have some good years first, before this stupid war got started? We're only young once. It isn't fair.

It was an old litany, one nearly as old as her marriage. It changed nothing. Nobody but Miriam heard it anyway.

She collected her purse and her mother's letter, then left for work.

~

May 25, 1944
My darling Del,

There hasn't been a soul in the drugstore all morning. I hate it when it's this quiet. It makes the days too long. It gives me too much time to think about you and wonder where you are and if you're safe.

I got the letter you sent before you left the States. I hope you're still in England, but Chief Jagger says, if you are, you won't be there long.

Everybody is talking that the end of the war in Europe can't be far off. Every time the newspaper or the radio reports a victory, I get excited. I think maybe it means you'll be coming home soon. When news came that Sevastopol fell to the Soviet forces two weeks ago and the Germans evacuated by sea, you'd think I knew where Sevastopol was.

School will be out soon, and Mother will be with me more hours in the store. Not that the help is really needed. We aren't doing much business. Not like we used to. I think we should open later and close earlier, but Dad said he didn't want us to do that. He said that, for as long as we can, we should help the folks in River Bluff feel like the war hasn't changed everything. So I guess I'm stuck working in the store more hours than I want to.

Del, you've got to stay safe and come home to me. There isn't going to be a baby. I found out this morning. I don't know if you wanted it to happen or not, but it didn't. So now you've just got to come back so we can have a family. You understand me, Del Tucker? You take care. You stay safe.

I didn't realize how lucky I was, your staying in the States for so long. I thought I understood, but I didn't. Now when I look at a newspaper or listen to the radio, when I read about or hear about another battle in Europe, I wonder if you're okay. And you've been gone only a few weeks. How will I make it for the duration? I feel as though you've already been gone an eternity.

I'm sorry, sweetheart. It seems I do nothing but complain in my letters. I don't mean to, and I know I shouldn't. You're the one in danger, not me.

I love you, Del. I don't think I knew how much until you went away this time. I love you with everything in me. I love you with my whole heart. I love you with my life. There isn't anything I want more than for you to come home and for us to be together and have a family and live like normal folk.

Remember how I used to think I wanted glamour and excitement? Remember when I ran away from home to become a movie star and

you had to come after me? But I don't want those things, Del. Honest,
I don't. All I want is you.

Stay safe, my darling.
Your loving wife,
Miriam

~

The bell over the shop door jingled, and Miriam looked up from
the stationery to see who had entered the store.

Bess Pritchett. Sally's mother.

Miriam felt a catch in her heart as she rose from the wooden
swivel chair. "Afternoon, Mrs. Pritchett."

"Hello, Miriam." The woman smiled, but there was no
cheer in her expression. She'd taken the loss of her son hard.

"How's Sally?"

"She's right enough. 'Course, she doesn't really understand
that her brother's never comin' home. She just knows Douglas
isn't here now and that all of us feel bad."

Miriam was sorry she'd asked. She didn't want to talk
about soldiers who never came home. "What can I help you
with, Mrs. Pritchett?"

"I need some ointment to help ease my husband's misery
a bit. His rheumatism's actin' up again."

"I've got something right over here that should help."
Miriam stepped from behind the counter and led the way.

The door opened again. "Ma?"

"Roy, I told you to wait in the car," Bess Pritchett answered
her son.

The little towheaded boy came into view at the end of the
aisle, holding a squirming ball of black-and-brown fur in his
hands. "He's whinin' for his ma. Can't we keep him?"

"No, son. Already told you we couldn't. Now you git on
back to the car."

The youngster looked at Miriam. "You want him?"

"Roy," Bess said sternly, "you mind me right now."

But Roy didn't mind. With all the stubbornness of a willful five-year-old, he marched toward Miriam and held out the puppy. "Here."

Even as she shook her head, Miriam took the tiny puppy. He squirmed in her hands, and she drew him against her chest. "What's his name?"

"Doesn't got one."

The puppy licked Miriam's chin, then nuzzled into the curve of her throat, making soft whimpering sounds. She could feel the rapid beating of his heart beneath her hands. "What kind is he?"

"Yorkshire terrier," Bess answered. "But don't trouble yourself about him. We're takin' the little runt to the pound 'cause we can't find him a home. Folks don't have time nor money to spare for fancy pets, and I just can't deal with—"

"No," Miriam said, making up her mind suddenly, "I'd like to keep him, if it's all right." She held the puppy away so she could look at his face. "I think I'll call you Sergeant York. Sarge for short." She glanced down at Roy. "What do you think? Is Sarge a good name?"

Roy nodded, grinning from ear to ear.

"How much, Mrs. Pritchett?"

"Well, I reckon he'd be free. We were givin' him to the pound anyway."

"Thank you." Miriam smiled as Sarge nibbled on her earlobe. She wasn't going to feel quite so lonely tonight.

~

P.S. Del, you'll never guess what I did a little while ago. I got myself a puppy. A little Yorkshire terrier that I've christened Sergeant

York after the character in the Gary Cooper movie that came out a few years ago. That's York for Yorkshire, of course, but I'm calling him Sarge. Rather patriotic, don't you think? Mrs. Pritchett was taking him to the pound because he's the runt of the litter and she couldn't sell him. The moment I saw Sarge, I knew I wanted him. Maybe because I can lavish some of the love I can't give to you in person onto him.

Does that make any sense? I hope it does. And I hope you'll like him when you see him. I hope he won't be too grown up before that happens. I hope you get to see him soon.

I'll have Mother take some pictures of Sarge and me with her Brownie camera so you can have them with you wherever you are. I'll get those for you just as soon as I can.

Now I'm taking this letter to the post office so it can be on its way to you. I'm sending all my love and devotion.

Be safe, my darling.

CHAPTER ELEVEN

"COME HERE, SARGE. YOU'RE GOING TO FALL IN IF YOU'RE NOT careful."

Miriam rescued the puppy from the riverbank. She ruffled his ears with one hand while holding him close.

"Silly dog."

It was amazing how quickly she'd become attached to Sarge. Only ten days since she'd carried home this tiny ball of fur to show her mother, and already the puppy had become a great comfort. Miriam might not sleep through the night without having to take Sarge outside to do his business, but neither was she sleeping alone. There was something soothing about feeling the puppy's small body nestled close to her own.

Miriam settled onto a boulder at the bend in the river. Still holding Sarge, she lay back and stared at the cloudless sky. The sun kissed her face, warming her skin, and her thoughts drifted as her eyes began to droop.

"Thanks be to God, which giveth us the victory through our Lord Jesus Christ."

Pastor Desmond had really worked up a lather this morning as he'd preached a sermon about victory.

"I believe in my heart that victory for the Allies is assured, whether that victory is next week, next month, or next year. It will come. But, my dear congregation, only the victory that comes with Christ will last. Until Jesus returns for His bride, as long as mankind rules the earth, there will be wars and rumors of war, for we are a fallen race."

Her father would have said, "Amen."

Miriam had been glad when church let out so she could get away by herself. She found her emotions stretched too thin whenever there was talk of the war. Everyone might say victory in Europe was close, that the Nazis were losing ground, that the war couldn't go on much longer. They might say it, but Miriam knew that plenty more men would die before it was done. And now that Del was there . . .

A shadow fell over her face, but before she could open her eyes, she heard a familiar voice. "I figured I'd find you here."

Releasing her hold on Sarge, who quickly scampered to the ground, Miriam sat up. "Jacob?" She stared at the tall, thin man beside the boulder, squinting at the sunlight behind him. "Is that *you?*"

"It's me." He chuckled. "In the flesh."

It wasn't until she was on her feet that she noticed his left arm was in a sling. "Jacob, you're hurt. You've been wounded."

"It's nothing."

She didn't believe him. "It must be *something* or you wouldn't be here."

"I have some recovering to do." He shrugged. "I'll be shipping out again in another month or two." He held out his good arm. "Doesn't the returning warrior get a hug from his favorite girl? Even if she is an old married lady?"

She punched his right shoulder. "Old married lady, my aunt Hattie." Then she hugged him tightly, hiding her face against his chest. "It's good to see you, Jacob."

Sarge whimpered and scratched at their legs with his front paws.

Jacob leaned back from Miriam and looked down. "What is that? A rat?"

"I beg your pardon. *That* is Sergeant York." She picked up the dog. "Unlike almost every other male I know, he's never going to run off to get shot at by the Nazis or Japanese. Are you, Sarge?" Tears filled her eyes, and she blinked madly to be rid of them.

Jacob put his right arm around her shoulder. "I heard about Del going overseas. I'm sorry, Miriam."

That was all the permission she needed. She turned her face to his chest once again and let herself cry.

~

Jacob recognized a broken heart when he saw one. He knew because he'd had one himself. He thought he'd never get over Miriam's marrying Del Tucker. Right up until he'd heard the news of their wedding, he'd held out hope that she'd change her mind.

"Seems like every time you and me are by this confounded river, you end up in tears. Wonder why that is?"

She sniffed.

"Come to think of it, you were gonna hate me forever 'cause I wouldn't marry you."

She looked at him, her pale cheeks streaked by tears. "It wasn't because you wouldn't marry me. It was because you wouldn't take me to Hollywood." She sniffed again. "That's why I was crying, and that's why I said I'd hate you."

"Oh, yeah. That's right." He winked. "Missed your chance to have the all-around best redheaded pilot in River Bluff for your husband, didn't you?"

She released a shaky sigh and returned his smile. "You're the *only* redheaded pilot in River Bluff, you idiot."

"Well, I'll be. You're right about that, too."

She elbowed him in the ribs, then moved away, clutching that silly dog to her chest. Jacob stood still, simply watching as she returned to the boulder where he'd found her minutes before. She sat on it, her back toward him, and he knew she was staring at the rushing waters of the river.

After a long while, she said, "Do you think he'll come back?"

More than anything in the world, Jacob wanted to comfort her, to promise that Del would be okay. But he couldn't lie—he'd watched men die, a couple of them in his own arms. War had taught him how fragile life is. They were here one minute and the next . . . blown to smithereens.

Miriam glanced over her shoulder. "Everybody says the Allies are winning in Europe, but that doesn't mean it'll be over soon, does it? In fact, it means they're going to push harder. Right?"

Jacob nodded.

"I don't think I'd want to live if Del doesn't come back." She turned toward the river again. "Sometimes it hurts too much to be in love."

"Yeah," he answered softly, "sometimes it does."

~

Later that afternoon, as Miriam and Jacob walked toward River Bluff, they saw Gard Holbright's dark green Ford bumping over the rutted tracks in the dirt road, coming toward them. Miriam quickly picked up Sarge.

Gard honked the horn twice as he rolled to a stop before them, then poked his head out the window. "Hello, Jacob. Somebody told me you were in town. Hello, Miriam. Have you two heard the news? The Allies have taken Rome."

Miriam turned toward Jacob, her heart in her throat. "Is this it? Is this what everybody's been waiting for?" *Is Del there? Is he in danger? Could a German be shooting at him right now?*

"No, this isn't the big push." He gave a slight shake of his head, then smiled. "But it's good news. Every victory for the Allies is good news."

"Are you coming to the church social tonight?" Gard asked Jacob. "Everybody's gonna want to hear what's happening in the

Pacific, and there'll be plenty of good cheer after today's news from Europe."

Jacob nodded. "Yeah, I plan to be there. The McAllister boys never miss the good cooking of the ladies of River Bluff if they can help it."

"Well then, see you there." Gard put his Ford in gear and drove away.

Jacob waited until the car was out of sight before asking Miriam, "Will you be at the social?"

"I suppose." Miriam set Sarge on the ground, then resumed walking. "Mother likes to go to all those things."

"But not you?"

She shrugged. "I don't know. It's okay, I guess. It's just . . ." She shrugged again and let her reply die, unfinished.

"It's just what?"

How could she explain to him that everybody else—her parents, her husband, her neighbors—seemed to get something from church that she didn't get? Everybody seemed so sure about God and heaven and hell and salvation and the whole works. Everybody except her. Del wanted her to find something more, but she didn't know what the *more* was or exactly how to find it. Del had found something profound. She'd seen it in his eyes, heard it in his voice. It wasn't that she didn't *want* to please him by finding the same thing. Only . . .

Jacob placed a hand on her shoulder. "Never mind. You don't have to tell me."

She tipped her head to the side, squeezing his hand between her ear and shoulder. "Thanks, Jacob. Thanks for being my friend."

"That's the easy part."

She glanced up, realizing with some surprise that he was different from the boy she remembered in her mind and heart. Back by the river, she'd simply seen Jacob, her childhood friend and confidant. But he'd grown up, become a man, a soldier. He'd changed, inside where it mattered most. He'd been through things she couldn't even imagine. She could see it written in his eyes.

"I was angry with you for joining up and going away, you know. Why'd you do it, Jacob? You and Del and Arledge. None of you waited until you *had* to go."

"You know the answer to that, same as I do."

"No." She peered at him. "I think there's another reason besides patriotism for you."

He frowned. "You think I'm not patriotic?"

"It isn't that. I just think there's more to it. You left so quick-like. You didn't even come to Boise to tell Del and me good-bye. I was awfully disappointed when I got back to River Bluff and found you gone."

She thought for a moment that he was going to reach out, halfway expected him to tuck her hair behind her ear, the way he'd done when they were teenagers. Instead, he shoved his hands into his pockets.

"I think I'd better get back to town. My dad's gonna be wondering where I got to." He took off with long, determined strides.

He sounded miffed. But why?

"Well? You comin' or not?"

Miriam had to run a few steps to catch up. "What's gotten into you?"

"Nothing."

Suddenly she understood, and laughter bubbled up from inside. "Why, Jacob McAllister, you're still sweet on me."

He kept right on walking, his gaze set on the road before him.

"I think that's about the nicest thing I've ever heard of," Miriam said.

He stopped. She did the same. When he looked at her, fire in his eyes—or was it passion?—her laughter died.

"I'm in no mood for teasing, Miriam."

A shiver raced along her spine.

"Let's just leave things be," he said, his voice low. "This isn't a game, and we're not kids anymore."

~

Eliza sank onto a wooden chair in the corner of the small stage at one end of the fellowship hall. It was the only available chair to be found. She'd never seen so many people crowded into All Saints Community Church, not even on Christmas or Easter. Nearly the entire population of River Bluff and the surrounding county had come to the church social. It seemed everyone wanted to celebrate the war news, as if they'd played a role in the Allies' march into Rome.

She supposed it was understandable. The country longed for good news. Everyone expected the invasion of Europe to happen soon. How could they help it? Even the newspaper had a daily column entitled "Invasion Weather," where they reported conditions in the Dover Straits.

O Lord, let the war end soon. Let there be an end to the killing and maiming.

A deep sigh escaped Eliza. She was weary to the bone. Her head pounded, and she felt oddly out of breath. Perhaps it was the warmth generated from so many bodies that made the air seem thin.

She fanned herself with a slip of paper she'd found in her pocketbook, all the while her gaze moving over the room, pausing briefly on familiar faces, people she'd known for a lifetime. It took her a few minutes to find her daughter. Miriam stood at the opposite end of the hall, Jacob McAllister at her side.

Jacob had been a gawky, not particularly good-looking youth, but now he appeared rather dashing in his Army Air Corps uniform, his carrot red hair trimmed short to his scalp. He'd changed, matured, in the years he'd been away from River Bluff. There was a new strength in the sharp angles of his face, a new breadth to his shoulders.

Eliza frowned. Miriam had been at loose ends in the weeks since Del's visit home. Miriam longed for her husband, and was obviously lonely and unhappy. It was a vulnerable place to be, especially for a vibrant young woman with a hunger to experience life.

And there was Jacob, who'd always worn his heart on his sleeve, looking at Miriam with those puppy-dog eyes of his. No longer a boy, he was a man in every sense of the word.

A man in love with a married woman. With Miriam.

Oh no!

Eliza's heart fluttered, and she pressed her fist against her chest.

Don't let them do anything foolish, Lord. Don't let them fall into temptation.

A wave of dizziness washed over her, and she closed her eyes, clasping her hands together in her lap.

I need Frank to come back. I'm tired.

Her skin vibrated over her bones. She touched her cheeks with her fingertips, as if that could stop the tingling.

I want my husband with me, Jesus. I need him at home.

She opened her eyes, but the room swam before her. The room and everyone in it was a blur of colors and strange shapes.

She was hot. Horribly hot.

What's happening to me, Lord?

That was her last thought before darkness overtook her, and she slipped from the chair in a dead faint.

CHAPTER TWELVE

WHILE MOST CITIZENS OF RIVER BLUFF SLEPT, MIRIAM TUCKER was among those few who heard the first official radio reports of the invasion of France. It was 1:32 in the morning, Mountain War Time, June 6, 1944.

"*At this moment,*" came the reporter's half-shouting voice amid the static, "*the greatest military undertaking in history is under way. America, we call upon you to pray for the sons and the fathers who are going over in a great wave of Allied manpower, attacking the Atlantic wall.*"

Miriam leaned toward her mother's bed. "Mother, do you hear? We've invaded Europe."

There was no response from Eliza. Not even the flicker of an eyelid.

"*Throughout last night and today, all England resounded with the thunder of RAF bombers and the big fleets of Flying Fortresses coming and going. While the Allied bulletin did not say exactly where the invasion was taking place, a report from Berlin said that Allied naval forces were shelling Le Havre, adding that the bombardment was terrific.*"

Del was part of the invasion. Miriam knew it without question. He was there, in the midst of the battle. Where exactly was Le Havre?

"*Just what element of surprise, if any, the landing troops achieved was not immediately announced by the supreme headquarters. There was no chance to hide the great convoys with only about five hours of darkness on the channel.*"

Was Del in the air or on the sea right now? Was he already in France?

"Although amphibious attacks are the most difficult in war, it's said that a quiet feeling of confidence has characterized the Allied generals all this week."

Miriam rose from her chair and walked to the window. Stars twinkled in a moonless night sky. The reporter droned on, but she ceased to listen.

"God, keep him safe. He trusts in You. If You'll keep him safe, I swear I'll trust in You, too."

Eliza moaned, and Miriam turned toward the sound.

The doctor had said it was a virus. Nothing to be overly concerned about. Just let the fever run its course and Eliza would be herself again.

Miriam was frightened anyway. Her mother looked gray and sunken. She wished her father were home. She'd put in a call to him earlier in the day, but he'd been at the plant. She could only hope he'd received her message and would phone soon.

She heard a soft rapping on the front door, and her heart jumped to her throat. Who was it? At this hour it could only be bad news.

What if—?

Her gaze darted to the radio.

"A shattering barrage such as reduced the defenders of the Mediterranean island of Pantelleria last summer was laid down by the combined air forces. Added to this barrage was the thunder of naval warships off the coast behind the advancing naval craft . . ."

The knocking grew louder. Fearfully, Miriam went to answer. She found Jacob on the opposite side of the door.

"Have you heard about the invasion?" He was unable to disguise his soldier's enthusiasm.

She nodded.

"I couldn't help it. I had to come. I took a chance you'd be awake. When I saw your light on—"

"I was listening to the radio."

"We're gonna lick 'em. Hitler's on the run now." Exuberantly, he grabbed her with his good arm and pulled her close for a tight hug. "We've got that dirty Nazi running scared. The war's gonna be over soon. You'll see." He gazed into her eyes. The excited smile faded. His voice dropped to a near whisper. "Things're gonna go back to the way they used to be."

Then he kissed her.

For a heartbeat or two, she let him. After all, this was Jacob, her best and dearest friend, who knew her better than almost anybody. Was it so terribly wrong to be held and kissed by a friend?

Then she thought of Del. Del, who was fighting for her somewhere overseas. Del, who loved her and trusted God and trusted her, too. Del, who would never hurt or betray Miriam.

She pressed her hand against Jacob's chest and gently pushed away. "Stop, Jacob."

They stared at each other for a long while. Regret, shame— a hundred emotions filled the room.

Finally, Jacob took another step backward. "I was out of line. I'm sorry. I wouldn't hurt you for anything."

"It's just that—"

"I understand."

She drew a shaky breath. "Do you suppose Del's okay?"

He pondered her question before answering. "The landing couldn't've been easy. The Germans have been fortifying their west wall for most of the last four years. Only time'll tell how bad it was for our guys."

"I'm scared, Jacob."

"I know you are. But you've gotta believe it'll be okay. That's all any of us can do now."

~

"Dad will be here by tomorrow night," Miriam said as she held the last spoonful of broth to her mother's lips.

Eliza dutifully opened her mouth and swallowed the clear liquid, although it took obvious effort to do so.

Miriam set the empty soup cup on the tray. "Would you like another sip of milk?"

Her mother turned her head in a gesture of refusal.

"Okay." Miriam reached for the lunch tray. "Is there anything more you need?"

"Read some more."

"What would you like to hear? A novel?" She looked for the book on the nightstand.

"The newspaper."

"The paper? But I already read you everything in it that's of any interest."

"The prayer."

"What—?"

"Read the prayer again."

"Oh."

Miriam reached for the *Idaho Daily Statesman* and opened it to page two. Under the headline "D Day Comes to Boise" she found the article. Churches in the capital city, it said, had planned services at intervals throughout the day. All would be repeating the same prayer.

"Read it again, Miriam." Her mother closed her eyes.

Miriam folded the paper in half, then in fourths, and dutifully began to read aloud: "'Almighty and most merciful God, Father of all mankind, lover of every life, hear, we beseech Thee, the cry of Thy children in this dark hour of conflict and danger. Thou has been the refuge and strength, in all generations, of those who put trust in Thee. May it please Thee this day to draw to Thyself the hearts of those who struggle and endure to the uttermost. Have mercy on them and suffer not their faith in Thee to fail.'"

Miriam paused. *"Suffer not their faith in Thee to fail."*

Del believed in God. Believed in Him in a way Miriam didn't. She'd seen the deep, abiding faith of her parents. She'd seen it in other members of the church. She'd seen it in Del when he came home last month. And although she couldn't quite fathom it, she knew that his faith in God would be her husband's strength and shield.

"Suffer not *his* faith in Thee to fail," she whispered.

Eliza's hand fell upon Miriam's knee. When their gazes met, her mother nodded in encouragement. Miriam smiled in return, then continued reading, her voice softer now, her mind lingering a bit longer over the words, allowing them to sink in, to take hold.

"'Guide and protect them by Thy light and strength that they may be kept from evil. May Thy comfort be sufficient for all who suffer pain or who wait in the agony of uncertainty. O righteous and omnipotent God, who in their tragedies and conflicts, judgest the hearts of men and the purposes of nations, enter into this struggle with Thy transforming power, that out of its anguish there may come a victory of righteousness. May there arise a new order that shall endure because in it Thy will shall be done in earth as it is in heaven.'"

Eliza whispered, "Yes, Lord. Let it be so."

"'Forgive us and cleanse us, as well as those who strive against us, that we may be fit instruments of Thy purposes. Unto Thy most gracious keeping we commend our loved ones and ourselves, ascribing unto Thee all praise and glory, through Jesus Christ, our Lord. Amen.'"

"Amen."

Feeling at peace for the first time in ages, Miriam lowered the paper to her lap.

"I believe I'll rest now," Eliza said.

Miriam nodded, then picked up the tray, rose from her chair, and walked toward the door. Still marveling at the sense of unexplainable calm that had overtaken her, she whispered, "I think I can rest now, too."

CHAPTER THIRTEEN

JUNE PLODDED STEADILY TOWARD JULY.

Frank Gresham came home to stay, having left his defense plant job in Portland, and Eliza's health improved under her husband's watchful eyes.

Jacob left River Bluff a week after D day. Some said he was called back to duty. Others said he'd simply grown restless. Miriam suspected she was the real reason—especially since he didn't tell her good-bye.

Miriam received five letters from Del, all written before the Normandy Invasion. Four families in the valley had lost loved ones on that longest day, but the Gresham home received no telegrams. Miriam breathed easier with every passing hour.

But maybe the reason for her calm wasn't because "no news is good news," as many said. Perhaps it was something else. Only what? She pondered that question as she knelt on the lawn, weeding morning glories from her mother's flower beds.

Why wasn't she frightened the way she used to be? It wasn't because of the war. Young men from around the world—including Del, Arledge, maybe even Jacob—continued to risk their lives for the sake of freedom in this bloody conflict. So what had changed?

She sat back on her heels, removed her gardening gloves, then swept her hair off her forehead with the back of her wrist. Overhead, whispery white clouds, like stretched cotton balls, trailed across the blue heavens. A summer breeze caused tree limbs to sway in a gentle dance.

"Why aren't I afraid like I used to be?"

Sarge scratched Miriam's thigh, drawing her attention.

"It's very strange." She lifted the puppy into her arms, letting him nibble her earlobe and nuzzle her chin.

She remembered the morning Del had told her he'd met Jesus. His remark had made her uncomfortable, even a little angry. All his life he'd gone to church, the same as Miriam. Yet what he'd seemed to be saying was that he'd found something she hadn't.

"*Has* he found something more?" She looked up again. "Is it You?"

She heard no voice from heaven. She received no miraculous sign from God. The only sounds were the rustling of leaves—and the rattle of Tuttle Ormsby's tri-wheeled mail cart as it rolled toward the Gresham home.

Miriam's gaze darted toward the front walk.

When Mr. Ormsby saw her sitting on the grass, he gave her one of his crooked grins and held up an envelope. "Got somethin' for ya, Miriam."

She put Sarge down and was on her feet in an instant.

"Looks t'me like it's from Del."

She ran toward him, her arm outstretched. When she had the envelope in her hand, she hesitated, afraid she would be disappointed, but when she found the courage to look, she recognized Del's bold handwriting.

Pressing the envelope to her chest, she closed her eyes. "Please be written after the sixth of June."

"You got a few more things here," Mr. Ormsby said, interrupting her prayerful whisper.

She looked at him, chagrined. "I'm sorry. Thanks."

The elderly man chuckled. "Don't stand there apologizing to me, young woman. Go read that letter from your husband."

She didn't say good-bye. She simply hurried into the house,

not stopping until she reached her bedroom. She dropped the rest of the mail onto the bed, then stared once more at the only envelope that mattered to her.

"Please."

She slipped her finger beneath the flap and tore it open. Breathing hard, as if she'd just finished a race, she removed, then unfolded the slip of white paper. Words and phrases seemed to jump off the page: *June 22 . . . leg wound . . . hospital in England . . . discharge . . . coming home . . .*

"Mother!" She darted from her room and into her parents' room. "Mother!"

Eliza, seated in a chair near the window, her basket of mending on the floor nearby, looked up with a startled gaze.

"It's Del!" Miriam waved the letter. "He's coming home! He's alive and he's coming home."

"Oh, thank God."

"He was part of the invasion of France, and he was wounded in the leg." She scanned the letter again. "He doesn't say how badly he's hurt, but he's in a hospital in England. He's going to be discharged soon. He's coming home for good."

"Thank You, O most merciful God," Eliza said softly.

"Yes, thank You, God." Miriam clutched the precious letter to her chest, threw back her head, and whirled in a tight circle. "Thank You, thank You, thank You."

Dizzy, she fell onto the bed, joyful laughter bubbling from deep inside her. She was deliriously happy. She wanted to shout her joy to the world. She wanted to run down the streets of River Bluff, proclaiming the news of Del's return.

She might have done so if her father hadn't arrived at that precise moment.

"Frank!" Eliza exclaimed. "Don't tell me it's the lunch hour already."

Miriam sat up. She opened her mouth to share Del's letter, but the words died in her throat.

Her father was holding a telegram, and his bereft expression said what he had yet to speak aloud.

"Frank?"

He nodded slowly.

Miriam turned toward her mother. Eliza's right hand was pressed against the base of her throat.

"Not our boy. Not Arledge."

Miriam looked at her dad again. "Arledge is dead?" she asked in disbelief.

Tears streaking his cheeks, he nodded a second time.

Why, God? If You could keep Del safe, why couldn't You do the same for my brother?

JULIANNA

SUMMER 2001

CHAPTER FOURTEEN

"How awful!" I said, my throat tight.

Jacob released a long sigh while smoothing the service cap over his thigh with one gnarled hand. "Yes, Miriam took it real hard. She felt guilty for quite a spell about Del livin' and Arledge dyin'. As if it was somehow her fault 'cause she didn't worry about her brother more."

I could understand such feelings.

"Mrs. Gresham never recovered her full health," Jacob continued. "I suppose it was partly because of losing her son. But her faith saw her through."

I wondered what would sustain me were I to lose my child. A terrifying thought! I was certain I'd be angry at God rather than comforted by faith in Him.

Leland had started going to church this past year, but I'd declined his invitations to go with him. Organized religion, as far as I could tell, was stuffy and old-fashioned and seemed pointless. Times changed. The world had grown up. Maybe the Christian church had its place in the past, but it wasn't relevant anymore.

Sally held out a hand toward Jacob, a silent request for the service cap. He obliged, placing it onto her upturned palm.

Softly, she said, "Miriam told me years later it was looking for answers about why Arledge died that caused her to finally surrender completely to the Lord. I wish my dad had had the same sort of experience after we lost Douglas. Dad needed God, but instead, he just got bitter."

"You're Sally Pritchett?" I blurted in surprise, I suppose because in my mind, Sally had remained a child.

She smiled. "Well, I've been Sally Farnsdale for nearly forty-seven years, but yes, it's me." As she spoke, she set aside the cap, then reached in and withdrew the soda-fountain glass.

"I remember the day we unpacked these." She had a faraway look in her eyes. "Seems like only yesterday."

MIRIAM

Autumn 1952

CHAPTER FIFTEEN

"It smells like it might snow." Miriam stared out the plate-glass window of the M&D Five & Dime. "I'm not ready for winter yet."

"Me, either," Sally Pritchett replied.

Miriam turned toward the lunch counter, where Sally was unpacking the soda glasses that had arrived earlier today. "Del might get caught in a storm."

"You know what, Mrs. Tucker? I hope I find me a husband just like Mr. Tucker and that he'll love me and I'll love him the same way as you two."

"Why, thank you, Sally." Miriam felt a pleased flush rise in her cheeks.

"I mean it," the girl continued. "Sometimes you'd think you were newlyweds, the way you are around each other." She laughed. "Not like most old married couples."

Old married couples? Miriam shook her head.

She supposed she must seem old to sixteen-year-old Sally. Miriam had turned thirty-one this past summer. Del was forty, his hair beginning to gray at the temples, a look she rather liked on him.

Sally set two more glasses into the sink. "So how long have you been married?"

"Eleven years this month." Even as she said it, Miriam could scarcely believe it.

Eleven wonderful years.

Eleven almost perfect years.

Almost.

The door opened, letting in a draft of crisp November air. "Hey, beautiful."

Oh, how the sound of Del's deep voice sent shivers of pleasure up her spine. She turned around.

His face was red from the cold, his hair disheveled by the wind. "Bet you were afraid I'd get caught in a storm." He arched an eyebrow. "Weren't you?"

Sally didn't give Miriam a chance to answer. "She sure was, Mr. Tucker. She hates it when you're gone."

He grinned, and Miriam wondered how an old married man of forty could still make her go weak in the knees with a smile.

"I wasn't the least bit worried," she lied, even as she hurried toward him to bury herself in his embrace.

He brushed his lips across the crown of her head. "I can never get home to you soon enough, sweetheart."

She tipped her head back, gazing into his eyes.

With his mouth a hairsbreadth from hers, Del whispered, "'Behold, you are beautiful, my love; behold, you are beautiful; your eyes are doves.'"

To which she replied, "'O that you would kiss me with the kisses of your mouth! For your love is better than wine.'"

He obliged, and she didn't even mind Sally's giggles.

When at last they parted, Miriam put her right arm around Del's back while taking his cane in her left hand. Together, they made their way toward the rear of the store.

"How did you find things?" she asked.

"Discouraging."

She pressed her head against his shoulder. "So why do you go?"

"You know why."

Yes, she knew. For the past six years, on the first and third

Tuesdays of every month, Del had been driving to Boise to visit veterans in the hospital and at the old soldiers home. Many of those men had no other visitors, no family or friends. Some would never be released from the hospital. A few had fought in the First World War, many in the second, and now there were more young men, fresh from the fighting fields of Korea.

Miriam wondered if mankind would ever be at peace with one another. But she knew the answer to that: *Not until Christ reigns over all the earth.*

Miriam knew there were times, although Del would have never confessed it to her, that he felt a measure of guilt for surviving the invasion of Normandy. The bullet that shattered his left thigh had left him with a permanent limp and ended not only his stint as a soldier but his career in law enforcement. But deep down, Del still believed he hadn't given enough, not when others had given all.

Of course, there were other reasons for his visits to those men. Better reasons. He went to share Christ's love. He went because he was called to go.

"And how was *your* day?" he asked, interrupting her musings. "Busy?"

"Not really. Dad came in for lunch, along with Mr. Holbright and Chief Jagger. Plenty of kids were in after school let out. Same group as always. Oh, we got that shipment of new glasses." She motioned with her head toward the counter. "Sally's unpacking them now. The order of dress patterns came in, too, but I'm waiting to sort through them until tomorrow."

"Tired?"

"Mmm."

"Why don't we send Sally home and close early?"

"Do you think we—"

"There's nothing for sale in here that won't keep until tomorrow. You said yourself it hasn't been busy." He tightened his arm around her shoulders. "I'll build a fire in the fireplace. We can snuggle up on the couch and listen to music on the radio."

She smiled. "It sounds delightful. I am rather tired."

Truth was, she'd been tired a lot lately. Some mornings it was nearly impossible to make herself get out of bed.

"Are you okay?" Del asked.

"Yes, honey. I'm fine. Let's close up shop and go home."

~

When Sally exited the five-and-dime at a quarter to six, she saw Hadley Abernathy walking toward her on the sidewalk. Her heart skipped a beat or two. When he waved at her, she flushed with pleasure.

"Hi, Sally. Getting off early?"

She nodded, hoping against hope it wasn't chance that had brought him there.

"Mind if I walk you home?"

She couldn't believe it. Her wish had come true! Hadley, the most popular senior boy at River Bluff High, was going to walk her home from work. Her, Sally Pritchett—a roach by anyone's definition, even her own. The popular crowd never noticed girls like her.

"Cat got your tongue?"

She blushed brighter. "No . . . I mean . . . yes. I mean . . . sure you can walk with me if you want." She stopped, shrugged, then attempted an I-couldn't-care-less toss of her head, and added, "It's a free country, isn't it?"

"Last time I looked." He laughed softly.

She could just *die!*

Sally started walking.

He joined her.

Hadley was not only the most popular senior at River Bluff High. He was also the best looking, the tallest, and the smartest. His folks were well-to-do, and he had his own car, a hot rod with flames painted along both sides. He was the star football player and the class president, and he could have any girl in River Bluff. Why he seemed to like her, Sally couldn't figure out, but he was always nice to her.

She, on the other hand, wasn't popular with the boys. Too thin and too flat-chested, she had mousy brown hair, and a too-long nose with a pointy end, like the witch in *The Wizard of Oz*. Her eyes were too big for the rest of her face, and her mouth was too wide, reminding her of a rainbow trout. Her folks didn't have much money, which was why she'd taken the after-school job at the M&D. A straight-A student, Sally wanted to go to college after she graduated, and if she was going to do that, she'd have to pay for it herself.

"You mad at me or something?" Hadley asked, the teasing sound still in his voice. "Slow down. Talk to me."

She glanced at him. "About what?"

"I don't know. School. Your job. Your little brother."

"Why would I want to talk about Roy?"

Hadley put his hand on her shoulder, bringing her to a halt at the corner of Main and Elm. When her eyes finally met his, he asked, "Want to know why I'm really here?"

She swallowed hard and nodded.

"I came to ask you to the harvest dance."

She must have looked plenty stupid, the way she stared at him in surprise. But she couldn't help herself. Nor could she find her voice.

"Will you?" he asked.

Sally had this sudden image of Mr. and Mrs. Tucker kissing by the front door of the store. She remembered exactly how Mr.

Tucker held his wife, the way her throat was arched, the splay of his fingers on her back.

What if Hadley kissed me like that?

"Will you go with me, Sally?"

She nodded again, still staring at him like the village idiot.

"Great." He grinned, then jerked his head toward the east end of town. "Come on. Let's get you home before it turns colder."

CHAPTER SIXTEEN

THREE TIMES A WEEK, FRANK GRESHAM JOINED THE TUCKERS FOR supper at their house. A widower of four years, Frank still hated to eat alone. They enjoyed his company, but Del was glad this wasn't one of those nights. He wanted Miriam to himself.

He turned the dial on the radio until he found the station, then faced the sofa where Miriam sat, her feet drawn up beside her. She smiled when their gazes met.

She does look tired.

Concern niggled at him as he walked across the living room. How long had those shadows been under her eyes? How long had she looked so pale?

Rosemary Clooney's voice, singing "Our Love Is Here to Stay," drifted from the speaker.

She's working too hard. That's all we seem to do these days. When was the last time we did something just for fun?

He settled onto the couch beside his wife, putting an arm around her shoulders and drawing her close. She released a sigh of pleasure as she rested her cheek against his chest.

"I love you, Miriam. Have I told you that lately?"

"Mmm. Yes, you have. But that's okay. Tell me again."

He stroked her hair. "I love you."

The fire on the hearth crackled, competing with Miss Clooney for attention.

"Jacob was in the store this morning," Miriam said after a brief while.

Del frowned. "What did he want?" It wasn't that Del didn't like Jacob. He was a good enough fellow, in his own way. But there was something about Jacob's friendship with Miriam that got under his skin.

"He wants to talk to you about increasing your life insurance." Miriam shifted position, turning to lie across his lap so she could look up into his face. "He says it's important you do it soon. Rates will keep going up now that you're past forty."

He scowled.

Miriam laughed.

"What?" Del said.

"I just remembered something that happened earlier at the store. Sally referred to us as an old married couple. That *old* part sort of caught me by surprise."

He cleared his throat and hunched his shoulders. "Well," he said, forcing his voice to quaver, "I am forty now, you know."

"Kiss me, you old fool."

"Gladly."

By the time the kissing was done, Miss Clooney was singing a new melody, "You Make Me Feel So Young." Del raised an eyebrow and looked over at the radio. "How did she know?" They both laughed.

"Maybe we ought to take a trip," Del suggested as Miriam snuggled close again. "Go to California. Maybe San Diego. Some place warm and sunny. Spend the whole winter there."

"We couldn't afford it."

True enough, but he didn't like hearing it. Maybe because he was getting older. Maybe because so many things had turned out differently than he'd planned on the day he married Miriam Gresham.

He felt a twinge of shame for his ingratitude.

Sorry, Lord.

He was richly blessed. He had Miriam for his wife. He had

a comfortable home and a business that provided for them both. It might not be the career he'd planned on. He might not be able to run a footrace with this bum leg of his. They might not have the children they'd both wanted. But he'd learned long ago that God's grace was sufficient. He only had to remember some of those vets in Boise to feel a fresh wave of remorse for his unspoken complaints.

"Del?"

"Hmm?"

"I don't need a vacation in sunny California. I only need you."

Oh yes. Del Tucker was richly blessed indeed.

~

"I'm going to Mooney's," Jacob shouted above the squalling of the baby and the squeals of the twins. "I need some peace and quiet so I can finish this paperwork."

"Fine," Elaine hurled back at him. "Run off like you do every night. We're used to it."

"It's my job." He slapped his hat onto his head. "This is what I do, Elaine. We've got rent to pay and three kids to feed. Remember?"

His wife was crying as she picked up Mac, their six-month-old son. "You're not going to Mooney's to work."

"At least over there a man can hear himself think." He stormed out of the house before he said something he'd regret.

It was snowing. Tiny, shardlike flakes blowing sideways in a blustery wind. But Jacob didn't bother to get the car. He leaned into the wind and strode into the night, hoping the chill would clear his head.

His home seemed always to be in a state of bedlam, some days worse than others. His wife never fixed herself up nice, the way she had before they got married. Their twin daughters, Victoria and Valerie—who'd turned five last March—were into mischief from the moment they woke up to the moment they went to bed, and Mac never seemed to stop fussing.

How'd this happen to me?

There he'd been, newly mustered out of the air corps in early 1946, playing the role of war hero and having a good time in San Francisco. That was where he'd met Elaine Cooper, a pretty blonde who, at the time, had reminded him a little of Miriam. Twenty years old and ready for a man of her own, Elaine had set her cap for Jacob. He should've seen it coming, but he hadn't. Just all of a sudden, he'd been engaged, and the next thing he'd known, he had a wife.

Nine months after that, he'd been the father of twins.

He muttered beneath his breath and walked faster, but he couldn't escape his racing thoughts. Hadn't he been good to Elaine? Hadn't he provided her with a nice house to live in? Okay, so they didn't own it, but it was still nice. Why couldn't she be content?

And why couldn't she maintain a little bit of order? Whatever happened to a man's home being his castle? Was it too much for him to ask to come home at the end of a hard day at work and enjoy a good meal and well-behaved children and some peace and quiet? Was it?

Elaine accused him of running away from life. Maybe that was true. But it wasn't the life he'd wanted in the first place. He couldn't even remember proposing to Elaine. More than once he'd suspected she'd tricked him into marriage, maybe when he'd had a little too much to drink. And it sure hadn't been his idea to have kids so quickly. They hardly got a chance to know each other as man and wife before the girls came.

As he crossed Cottonwood Street, he glanced toward Del

and Miriam's house, wishing he could go talk to Miriam. She had a way of making sense of things.

Lucky Del. Going home each night to a beautiful wife and a quiet home. The worst thing Del had to deal with was walking Sarge, that silly little terrier of Miriam's.

Okay, so he wasn't being fair. The Tuckers hadn't exactly had it easy. They'd had plenty of hard knocks, he supposed, yet they were still the two happiest people he knew.

Peace, Miriam called it. Peace from knowing Christ.

Jacob grunted. He never would have figured her to be the one to get religion. Sure, her folks had always been churchgoing, like the McAllister clan, but that hadn't stopped Miriam from doing what she wanted as a girl. She'd been headstrong, stubborn, and fun loving, and Jacob had liked her that way.

If things had been different, if she'd felt the same way about him as he had about her, maybe . . .

He arrived at Mooney Tucker's house then and promptly put away all thoughts except for sharing a few beers with his boss and forgetting his troubled lot in life.

CHAPTER SEVENTEEN

"YOU'RE LOOKING KIND OF PEAKED, PIXIE."

Miriam frowned at her dad. "Thanks a lot. I needed to hear that." She shook her head. "When are you going to stop calling me that silly pet name?"

"Never. Now tell me what ails you."

"Just a queasy stomach." She stared at the drugstore shelves. "What do you recommend?"

Frank came out from behind the counter. "Well, let's have a look." He headed toward the front of the store. "Are you and Del still planning to chaperone the dance at the school tonight?"

"Yes."

"If you're sick, you ought to stay home."

Miriam gave him an I'm-not-a-little-girl-anymore-so-stop-treating-me-like-one look. "I'm not sick, Dad. I ate something that didn't agree with me. That's all."

"Hmm." He might as well have said he didn't believe her.

"Men," she muttered, remembering how Del had fussed over her that morning, saying she looked exhausted and should stay home and rest. Good thing she hadn't upchucked until after he left for the store.

She wasn't sick. If she were, she'd feel lousy all the time, and she didn't. She was listless, true, and had been for a few weeks, but today was the first her stomach had been upset. Otherwise, she felt fine.

"Here. This ought to do the trick."

"Thanks." She took the small bottle from him without looking to see what it was.

"You go home and lie down for a while. Let it work."

"Okay, Dad," she said with a sigh of resignation. "You win."

He chuckled as he placed his arm around her shoulders. "At least you don't have to worry about fixing Sunday dinner for your old man. I've been invited to dine with the Hogans tomorrow at their place."

She looked at him and grinned. "That'll be nice. You and Mr. Hogan haven't swapped stories in ages." Her reference was to the legendary but friendly competition between the two avid fishermen.

"Jim's got kin visiting from Oregon," Frank replied, ignoring her teasing comment, "so it sounds like it'll be a houseful. Kind of an early Thanksgiving, I guess."

Miriam gave him a squeeze. "Well, I hope you'll have a great time."

"We will. Now, you get on home. If you're going to chaperone a bunch of teenagers, you need to be in tip-top form. There's bound to be at least one like you in their midst."

"Was I so bad?"

In a dry tone, he answered, "Yes."

She laughed, gave him another hug, then left the drugstore, pulling her coat collar up to keep out the cold.

As she walked home, she thought about her dad's comment. It was true. She had been a troublesome teen. She must have given her parents plenty of gray hairs.

She felt a sting of missing. For her mother. For Arledge. For the family they'd once been. And for the family she didn't have, for the children she'd wanted.

How she'd railed at God when the doctor told her it was doubtful she'd ever conceive. She'd been new in her faith that summer and so certain that being a Christian meant life would

be perfect. She'd cried when the doctor delivered his verdict.
Later she'd screamed at God, demanding that He give her the
babies she longed for. Didn't she and Del belong to Him?
Didn't the Bible say that children were a blessing? Why would
He withhold such a blessing from two of His own?

"The good Lord doesn't owe you an explanation," her
mother had told her at the time.

Those weren't words Miriam had accepted with grace. She'd
fought their truth for a long, long time.

*But You've given me a love for children, Lord, and I'm thankful.
Help me to be an example to others. Let me be there to listen and coun-
sel when a parent might not be heard.*

Lately, Miriam had given some thought to getting a college
degree. Her mother had been a wonderful teacher, such a
tremendous influence on young lives. Perhaps teaching children
was where God was calling her.

Is it, Lord?

She knew Del would support her if that was what she wanted.
He wouldn't ask where the money would come from for her tuition.
He'd simply work harder, dig deeper, do whatever was needed.

A wave of nausea caused her to stop walking and cover her
mouth with one gloved hand. For a moment or two, she feared
she'd be sick right there. Her eyes watered and the bile burned
the back of her throat.

*What if something's terribly wrong with me? Like Mother. What
if—?*

She swallowed hard, then hurried onward, eager for her
home, her bed, and a dose of the medicine her dad had given her.

~

"You won't be sorry you did this." Jacob stuffed the signed
papers into his briefcase.

"I hope not," Del answered, thinking about the additional premiums to pay every quarter.

"It's extra peace of mind. If anything happens to you, Miriam'll be financially secure. Remember, insurance is never a waste if you have it, but it's always a tragedy when you don't."

"You're a born salesman. You know that?"

"I'll take that as a compliment." Jacob rose from his chair. "Miriam's not in the store today?"

"No, I told her to rest up for tonight."

"What's tonight?"

The two men headed for the door of the cramped office in the back of the five-and-dime.

Del answered, "The harvest dance at the high school."

"Couple of suckers, that's what you are. You don't even have kids, and you stick yourselves with a bunch of teens on a Saturday night. You won't catch me doing stuff like that until I'm forced to."

Something—a quiet urging in his spirit—caused Del to reach out and place his hand on Jacob's shoulder, stopping him before he opened the office door. "Is everything all right with you?"

"Yeah." Jacob scowled. "What wouldn't be all right?"

"I don't know. You seem . . ." He shrugged, letting the explanation die unfinished.

For a moment, Jacob's facade slipped a bit, giving Del a glimpse of hidden pain and anger. Then the mask snapped back into place.

Jacob grinned. "You worry too much, Del." He yanked open the office door. "Tell Miriam hi for me. Hope the two of you have a good time at the school, but I still say you're crazy." He waved without looking back over his shoulder. "I'll bring you the policy when it comes in."

Del remained in the office doorway, watching as Jacob made

his way down the center aisle, greeting people as he went, smiling and looking happy.

But it was all an act, Del realized. Jacob's jocular manner was part of his salesman persona. Inside, he was hurting. He wondered if Jacob talked to Miriam about his unhappiness.

Maybe he should ask her.

~

Sally stared at her reflection in the mirror and wanted to cry. For some reason, she'd thought this dress and the two hours she'd spent that afternoon at Patty's Pinups, getting a new hairdo, would transform her into a beauty queen. They hadn't.

Why can't I be prettier? Hadley was going to take one look at her and break their date. She knew it.

She still hadn't figured out why he'd turned his attentions to her. Up until last month, she hadn't thought he'd known she existed. Now he spoke to her in the halls at school, and he was taking her to the harvest dance.

What if I step on his toes? What if I trip and fall?

"Sally!" her mom called from the living room. "Your young man's here."

She was mortified. It was absolutely deathsville. How could her mom call Hadley Abernathy her young man, right in front of him?

With her hands clenched, she walked out of her bedroom, praying silently that she wouldn't make a complete fool of herself before the night was over.

~

"Care to dance, Mrs. Tucker?" Del whispered in Miriam's ear when a familiar slow melody began to play.

"I'd love to."

The high school gymnasium was decorated with dried cornstalks, bales of hay, and plenty of orange pumpkins. In the dimmed lights, it looked festive. But no amount of decorating could change the poor acoustics or remove that faint scent of sweaty gym socks.

"You're the prettiest girl at the dance, Miriam Tucker."

She smiled. "And you're, like, the most."

Del laughed aloud, drawing the gazes of several young couples dancing nearby.

Miriam turned her head and placed her cheek against his shoulder. Through half-closed eyes, she watched pairs of students moving around the gym floor in time to the music. She knew most of them, either from church or the soda fountain at the five-and-dime. She'd baby-sat a few of them when she was a teen and they were in diapers, a fact she wouldn't hesitate to use if she needed to put some in their places.

Cruel, but effective.

She caught sight of Sally Pritchett and Hadley Abernathy, dancing nearby.

BEHOLD, SATAN DEMANDED TO HAVE YOU, THAT HE MIGHT SIFT YOU LIKE WHEAT.

Miriam felt a disquiet as the words came to her heart.

What are You telling me, Lord?

She lifted her head from Del's shoulder, continuing to watch Sally and Hadley. The girl looked nervous, a bit stiff and unsure of herself—and totally captivated by the boy who held her. Hadley, on the other hand, wore an air of confidence. And something else. Something she couldn't quite define. Something almost . . . predatory.

Miriam shuddered. *Keep Sally safe, Father.*

"Honey?" Del said softly. "You okay?"

"Yes," she replied without taking her eyes from the young couple.

"Hey, remember me?" Her husband's arm tightened.

She looked at him then. "Does it surprise you that Sally's here with the Abernathy boy?"

"Should it?"

"I don't know." She glanced over Del's left shoulder at the pair in question. "I just don't know."

CHAPTER EIGHTEEN

"Mommy!" Victoria screamed. "Val pulled my hair."

"She pulled mine first!"

From her bedroom, Elaine called, "Vicky, Val, behave yourselves."

There were a few moments of silence, then a bloodcurdling screech ripped through the McAllister household.

Jacob muttered some vile words he'd learned in the service, then rose from his easy chair and stormed toward the children's bedroom.

"What's going on in here?" he bellowed, slamming the door against the wall as he entered.

His red-haired daughters released their hold on each other and jumped back.

"I swear, I'll tan your backsides until you can't sit down for a month of Sundays."

"But she—"

"I didn't—"

He took a threatening stride forward, arm raised. "Shut up, the both of you!"

They burst into tears just as their mother entered the bedroom.

"Jacob, what are you doing?" She hurried toward the weeping girls.

"I'm restoring a bit of order. That's a father's job, isn't it? You sure don't do it."

Elaine stopped and spun about. For a heartbeat, she stared at him, wide-eyed. Then her expression went cold. "Since when have you acted like a father?"

The urge to strike his wife was nearly overwhelming.

She must have seen it, for she said, "Go ahead. Hit me."

Resentment burned hot and furious. He resented Elaine for all of his unrealized dreams, for everything that had gone wrong in his life.

"Why don't you get out, Jacob? Go drink with your boss. Why stay around here and make all of us miserable, too?"

He felt his lip curl. "Maybe I should get out for good."

"Yes," she said, "maybe you should."

That took Jacob by surprise. Then his anger returned, even hotter than before. He longed to call her a string of names that would express everything he felt.

More softly, she said, "There's a suitcase under the bed. Why don't you pack your things?"

"Don't tempt me."

"I don't mean to tempt you, Jacob. I'm telling you to leave. I want a divorce."

Those words hit him like a sucker punch. "Elaine, I—"

"Why torture yourself any longer?" she said with no emotion, no sign of tears. Nothing. "Why torture the kids and me? You don't like being a family man, so why pretend?"

He glanced at the twins. They stared at him with frightened, confused expressions. "I never said I don't like being a family man. I—"

"Yes, you did." Elaine sighed. "You've said it in a thousand different ways."

He wasn't a perfect husband or father. He'd never claimed to be. But divorce?

"I'm sure you can bunk over at Mooney's for a night or two. Or maybe Frank Gresham would let you stay with him." Her voice faltered as she turned away, saying, "Or you could always see if Miriam would take you in."

He followed her out of the children's room. "Elaine, let's be reasonable."

She didn't say a word. Just walked into their bedroom, knelt on the floor, and pulled a battered brown suitcase from beneath the bed. She rose again and placed it on the mattress. Then she met his gaze. "Whatever you don't take now you can get later."

"For crying out loud, Elaine. It's Sunday afternoon. I can't go barging in on people and tell them I need a place to stay. This is my home!" He threw up his arms in frustration.

"Your home?" She stepped toward him, fire replacing ice. "When have you treated it like a home? When was the last time you wanted to spend time with me instead of Mooney or one of your other drinking buddies? I'm not the baby-sitter. I'm your wife!"

He leaned forward. "Well, you won't be my wife if we get a divorce."

"Good."

He swore.

The ice returned. "You'll need a warm coat. It's going to snow some more." She walked past him. "Lock the door on your way out."

~

Grace Finch called on the pretext of discussing the All Saints Community Church's Christmas pageant. But it wasn't long before she got around to her real purpose.

"Have you heard the news, Miriam? Elaine McAllister threw Jacob out this afternoon. Theodora told me he's staying with her and Mooney for a few days. I don't suppose he knows where he'll be living after the divorce goes through. Poor Theodora. As if she needed that young man underfoot. I know you've always been friends with Jacob, but really. Why, the way he . . ."

Miriam stopped listening as Grace droned on.

Jacob, what have you done?

She knew he hadn't been happy lately, but she'd had no idea things had deteriorated to this level. A divorce? Those poor children. Poor Elaine.

Miriam's heart ached.

"Well, if my husband acted like that, I would—"

"I'm sorry, Mrs. Finch. I've got to hang up now. Thanks for calling. I'll get back to you about the pageant. Good-bye."

She set the handset in its cradle, knowing she'd been rude but not caring. If she'd had to listen to one more word of gossip, she would have said something she shouldn't. She knew she would have.

Miriam crossed the kitchen and stared out the window over the sink into the backyard, but her thoughts went much further, back through the years. So many memories of Jacob, some warm and wonderful, some poignant.

They'd weathered their momentary error in judgment on D day. Neither of them had mentioned the unfortunate kiss they'd shared. It was better left forgotten. Besides, with both of them happily married, there'd been no reason to give it another thought.

Only, the McAllisters weren't happy. That had been apparent for a long while now.

"Jacob, don't throw it away," she whispered. "You'll always be sorry. God gave you a family. Don't throw it away."

"It's not a good sign when you start talking to yourself, honey."

She turned around, leaning her backside against the sink and crossing her arms over her chest.

Standing in the kitchen doorway, Del stopped smiling when he saw her expression. "What is it?"

"I just got off the telephone with Mrs. Finch."

"And . . . ?"

"She said Elaine threw Jacob out of the house this afternoon. He's staying with Uncle Mooney and Aunt Theodora for the time being. She said they're getting a divorce."

Del whistled softly between his teeth. "That bad?"

"I don't know what to do—" she lifted her hands in a gesture of confusion—"or should I do anything?"

Her husband didn't offer a suggestion. He simply watched and waited.

Miriam turned toward the window again. "Those children. What will happen to them if their parents go through with a divorce? How will Elaine manage?"

Del's hands alighted on her shoulders. "Let's pray for them. Let's ask God what He wants us to do to help our friends."

"I need to ask for forgiveness, too." She pressed the side of her head against the back of his hand. "I hung up on Mrs. Finch."

Del chuckled as he leaned closer and kissed her cheek. "I'm sure He's already forgiven you, sweetheart. After all, you're only human."

~

Miriam did pray. She prayed with Del, and she prayed alone. She prayed briefly, and she prayed long and hard. She prayed as she went about her daily life, and she prayed on her knees beside her bed. But after three days, she still couldn't say she'd received a clear direction from the Lord.

The rumor about town was that Jacob had been seen every night that week at the roadhouse west of town. "Sloshed to the gills" was the descriptive term she'd heard. Her heart ached for her friend every time she thought of him, which was frequently.

Equally disturbing to Miriam was listening to Sally as she

went on and on about Hadley. To hear the girl describe him, he was Gregory Peck, Errol Flynn, and Marlon Brando, all rolled into one. He was handsome. He was smart. He was considerate. He was perfect in every conceivable way.

Miriam had no reason to believe that any of that wasn't true. Except for the words of warning that still echoed in her heart: BEHOLD, SATAN DEMANDED TO HAVE YOU, THAT HE MIGHT SIFT YOU LIKE WHEAT.

"My parents are letting me go with Hadley to Boise on Saturday," Sally said as she dried a glass bowl and put it on the shelf with the rest. "There's an exhibition game at the college and a dance afterward."

The feather duster stilled in Miriam's hand as she stared across the aisle at the teenager. Trying to quell the sick feeling in her stomach, she said, "That will get you home awfully late, won't it?"

"Yes, but since I'll be with Hadley, Mom said it would be okay this once."

"The roads could be icy. We might get more snow before the weekend."

"Hadley's a good driver. He won't let anything happen to us." SIFT YOU LIKE WHEAT . . .

"You worry too much, Mrs. Tucker. You get just like this when Mr. Tucker goes to Boise. I promise to tell Hadley to drive slow if the weather's bad. Okay?"

It wasn't Hadley's driving that had Miriam concerned. There was something about that boy . . .

~

Sally smiled to herself as she remembered Hadley's parting kiss last night. They'd stood on the sidewalk, out of reach of the porch light's glow. Sally had shivered in the cold, despite her coat.

"Here," Hadley had said. "Let me keep you warm."

He'd opened his coat, then closed it around her, drawing her against him.

She really hadn't been any closer to him than when they'd danced together. Yet it had seemed very different to Sally. Thrilling. Frightening.

She wouldn't have admitted it to Hadley, but she'd never been kissed before. She hadn't known at first what he meant to do when he'd lowered his mouth toward hers. She'd looked at him, her head tipped back. Then he'd kissed her.

Sally closed her eyes, reveling in the memory. She hadn't known a kiss could be like that!

I love you, Hadley Abernathy. I'd do anything to make you love me, too.

"Sally . . ."

Miriam's voice drew her unwillingly from her reverie.

"Remember when you told me you wanted to get married to someone who would love you the way Mr. Tucker loves me?"

It was kind of spooky. As if Miriam had read her thoughts or something. "Sure, I remember."

Miriam sat down on one of the stools and leaned toward Sally. "You understand that it's hard work, don't you?"

"What is?"

"Love."

Sally frowned. How could love be hard work? It wasn't hard with Hadley. She just loved him, and it made her feel warm all over. Warm and . . . scared.

"Do me a favor, Sally."

"What?"

"Remember that we have to live with the decisions we make. No matter how innocent our intentions, there are always consequences, good or bad, one or the other."

"I don't know what you mean."

Miriam took Sally's hand. "Maybe not now. But there'll come a time when you will, and when it comes, remember that God doesn't allow us to be tempted beyond what we can withstand. He'll provide a way of escape for His own if we but listen."

"Fiddlesticks, Mrs. Tucker. You're starting to sound like our pastor." Sally withdrew her hand.

"Maybe so. But, Sally—"

"I think I'd better get those shelves stocked now. Excuse me."

Sally hurried toward the back of the store, not certain what Miriam Tucker had been trying to say but positive she didn't want to listen.

CHAPTER NINETEEN

SECRETLY, MIRIAM PRAYED FOR A MAJOR BLIZZARD TO ROLL
through the county before Saturday morning, closing roads and
keeping folks at home—Hadley Abernathy and his hot rod in
particular. What happened instead was a warming trend, with
temperatures reaching into the high fifties, the heavens clear and
blue.

But Miriam forgot all about her prayer request when Del
served her breakfast in bed. On the tray, between the glass of
orange juice and a plate of pancakes, was her anniversary present.
She opened the velvet box to discover a beautiful heart-shaped
pendant with a small diamond-studded cross in its center.

"Oh, darling. It's exquisite." She looked up to meet his gaze.

"Not as exquisite as you are." He placed one knee on the
mattress. "Here. Let me put it on you."

Miriam leaned forward as Del took the necklace from its
box. In only a moment, he had the clasp fastened. She fingered
the pendant, thinking how very blessed she was to have this man
as her husband.

"How does supper at the Cliff Dweller sound?" Del asked as
he settled onto the bed beside her.

"Wonderful. Except the prices are outrageous."

"Miriam, let's do this." He nuzzled her right earlobe. "Our
anniversary only rolls around once a year."

Gooseflesh rose along her right arm, and she shivered with
pleasure. "All right. You win." She gave him a playful push. "But

131

let me eat my breakfast or we'll never get the store open on time."

"Hmm. Maybe that's what I had in mind."

~

"What was that about?" Del asked as Miriam hung up the telephone shortly after twelve-thirty that afternoon.

"It was Dad. He's too busy to come over for lunch, so he asked if I'd bring him something."

"He needs to hire more help."

"I know." She shrugged. "Deep down, he knows it, too, but he's too stubborn to admit it. I think he's afraid it'll be like saying he's old."

Del gave her a wry grin. "From where I'm sitting, fifty-six doesn't look so old."

Miriam laughed softly as she headed for the lunch counter.

A short while later, she took a towel-covered plate over to the drugstore, entering through the back door. She greeted Lou, the part-time pharmacist, then set the plate on the desk.

"He's out front," Lou said.

She nodded as her gaze scanned the store. She found her dad in the far left aisle. She was already walking in his direction before she caught sight of his customer.

Jacob McAllister.

Over her dad's shoulder, her gaze met with Jacob's. Despairing eyes, empty, hopeless. Sorrow filled her heart.

Give me the right words, Lord.

"Hello, Jacob."

He murmured her name, swaying slightly, then righting himself.

He's been drinking.

Giving herself a moment to gather her thoughts, she looked

at her dad. "I brought you a tuna salad sandwich. It's on your desk."

"Thanks, pixie." Understanding in his eyes, Frank patted her shoulder, then said to Jacob, "That all you need?"

Jacob nodded.

"Then if you'll excuse me." He left the two of them together at the front of the store.

"Guess you heard about me and Elaine."

"Yes, I heard. I'm awfully sorry. I . . . I wanted to come see you, but I didn't know what to say."

"Elaine should have that problem." His words were tinged with bitterness. "Unfortunately, she always has something to say."

Miriam reached out, placing her fingers on his forearm. "The situation isn't hopeless unless you let it be. Maybe if you and Elaine went to see Pastor Desmond or another minister, you could—"

"The marriage is over. It's been over almost from the start."

"How can you say that? You have three children."

He shook off her touch. "Having children doesn't mean a marriage is working. Besides, I don't love her."

"Love can be a choice, Jacob," she said softly. "You can choose to love Elaine if you want."

"That's just it," he replied, lowering his voice to match hers and leaning toward her at the same time. "I don't want. And I can't have what I do want."

In his alcohol-glazed eyes, Miriam saw something she'd chosen not to see in recent years. She'd wanted her best friend back in her life, so she'd pretended she couldn't see what was there. She'd pretended so well that she'd blinded herself to the truth.

What was it she'd said to Sally a few days before? Something like, no matter how innocent the intentions, there are always consequences, good or bad, for every choice, every action.

Suddenly, she was angry, more with herself than with Jacob. She slapped him. Hard. He stiffened and drew back, eyes wide.

"You're a stubborn, stupid, irritating fool." Her voice shook with rage. "You don't know how lucky you are or what you're throwing away." She shook her finger at him, as if he were a delinquent child. "You're like a horse, trying so hard to get that green shoot of grass on the other side of the fence, when you're standing right smack-dab in the middle of knee-high alfalfa."

"Miriam, I—"

"Let me make something perfectly clear. You and I have never been and could never be anything but friends. Even if I wasn't in love with my husband, which I am and always have been, you and I would only be friends. Why couldn't you see that? Are you really that blind?"

"But—"

"Do what's right for a change, Jacob. For your own sake and the sake of your family. Quit acting like a spoiled brat."

Without a backward glance, she turned on her heel and strode out of the drugstore.

~

Sally thought the day had been about as perfect as it could be. Riding in Hadley's hot rod. Spending the afternoon amid excited football fans. Being referred to as "Hadley's girlfriend." Supper at the Royal, the nicest restaurant in Boise. And now the drive home, with stars twinkling overhead and Hadley's right arm draped over her shoulders.

It was like a wonderful dream.

He knows I love him. And he loves me too. I can tell by the way he looks at me, by all the times he's kissed me.

The hot rod slowed.

"Sit up a second, baby," Hadley said, taking his arm from

around her shoulders, then gripping the steering wheel with both hands.

The automobile jerked forward, then slowed again.

"What's the matter?" Sally asked.

"Not sure. I'd better pull over and check it out."

A moment later, the hot rod rolled onto a gravel crossroad, following it down a gentle slope. At the bottom of the hill, Hadley turned off the engine—or did it die on its own?—and the headlights went out. Darkness enveloped the car, as did a chill.

"Hadley?"

"It's okay. I've got something in the back to keep us warm. You know, for emergencies. I'm sure the engine just needs to rest a bit. This one's sort of temperamental sometimes."

Sally shivered. "Shouldn't you get out and have a look?"

"Not yet." He reached behind the seat and retrieved a blanket, spreading it over them both. "Better get you warm first." He put his arm around her shoulders and pulled her close.

She came stiffly.

"Hey, baby. Relax. You've got nothing to worry about as long as you're with me."

Of course she didn't. He wouldn't let anything bad happen. He loved her, same as she loved him. Hadley would take care of her.

Beneath the cover, he stroked her arm. Slow, soothing strokes. Then he kissed her.

It was okay at first. She liked his kisses. Then something changed. Something subtle and indefinable, but a change all the same. Sally's heart pounded, her pulse raced.

"Ah, baby," Hadley whispered, "you make me crazy."

"There are always consequences, good or bad."

The memory of Miriam's words caused Sally to draw back from Hadley, but he wouldn't allow her to go far. His arms tightened, bringing her close again. Kissing her. Touching her. Making her feel like a queen instead of a roach.

In her mind, she saw Mr. Tucker kissing Mrs. Tucker, saw the tenderness, the love, the devotion. This wasn't the same.

She turned her head away. "Stop."

"Oh, come on, Sally. You want this as bad as I do. Don't hold out on me now." He placed his lips next to her left ear and whispered, "Nobody says no to me, baby. Not to Hadley."

A sick feeling twisted her stomach. Tears threatened, but she swallowed them back. "I'm not your baby. Get the car started and take me home."

"Hey, we got a couple hours before your mom said you had to be back." There was a hint of anger in his tone. "What's the hurry? Didn't I show you a good time today? Didn't I take you to the harvest dance? There were plenty of other girls I could've asked instead. Come here and show me how grateful you are. Come on and—"

GET OUT!

The words in her heart seemed like a shout, too strong not to obey. With a jerk of the door handle and a hard push, the passenger door was open, and Sally scrambled out into the inky night.

"What the—?"

Sally moved as quickly as she could in the direction of the highway.

"Are you crazy?" Hadley shouted.

"Not anymore," Sally answered as she climbed the hillside, but she was speaking to herself rather than to him.

～

Miriam and Del didn't go to the Cliff Dweller for supper. They didn't go anywhere for their anniversary. They stayed home, where Del could hold Miriam while she cried and poured out her heart.

"I was cruel to him," she whispered finally. "I could have been gentle. I could have tried to show him the more excellent way, like the Bible says. Instead—" her voice caught on a sob— "I . . . I slapped him."

Del wouldn't mind knocking Jacob up alongside the head a time or two himself, but he didn't say so to Miriam.

"I slapped him right there for all the customers in the drugstore and anybody walking down Main Street to see. Oh, the gossips must be having a heyday right now."

"Don't you worry—they'll have something new to talk about tomorrow."

"However will I face Elaine? I'll have to sometime, but what can I say to her?"

"The failure of their marriage isn't your fault, hon."

In a quavering voice, she replied, "No. But maybe I could have helped save it if only I'd realized what Jacob was thinking."

Del kissed her on the forehead. "Why don't we go see her tomorrow after church? Together. Maybe we can still help. You never know."

Tears welled in her eyes. "Thanks for understanding," she said softly. "Thanks for loving me."

"That's the easy part, sweetheart. That's the easy part."

CHAPTER TWENTY

MIRIAM SCARCELY HEARD THE PASTOR'S SERMON. SHE WAS TOO busy anticipating their call to the McAllister home. She kept imagining different scenarios, ways that she and Del might help bring the estranged couple together.

The congregation rose to sing the closing hymn. Miriam reached for the hymnal. The church organ hit a sour note, and when Miriam looked up, the sanctuary swam before her eyes. She thought she heard Del say her name, but she couldn't be certain for the sudden whirring sound in her ears. Then everything went black.

She awakened in the aisle to find Dr. Carson's kindly old face smiling down at her. "Here she is," he said.

Del leaned over her next. "You scared the living daylights out of me, sweetheart."

"And me," she heard her dad say, although he was out of her line of vision.

"Sorry." She tried to rise, but a hand on her shoulder kept her down.

"Not yet, Miriam," Dr. Carson said. "I want to know why you fainted before I let you go home." He looked at Del. "Let's get her to my office."

"Such a lot of fuss over nothing," she protested—to no avail.

~

Jacob nearly turned and left before Elaine opened the front door in answer to his knock. Once she saw it was him, he thought she might slam it in his face.

"Can we talk?" he said quickly.

She frowned. "What about?"

"Can I come in first? It's kinda cold out here."

"I guess it's okay." She stepped back, begrudgingly giving him entrance.

Jacob glanced into the living room. "Where're the kids?"

"The girls went to church with the neighbors. Mac's sleeping." She massaged her forehead with the fingertips of one hand. "What do you want, Jacob?"

"I want another chance."

Her eyes widened. Her mouth thinned.

"Look, Elaine, I know I've made a royal mess of things, and I'd understand if you wouldn't let me back. But I'm asking you to, all the same."

"Why?"

"Well, for one thing—" he looked at the floor—"a wise friend pointed out that I was actin' like a spoiled brat and didn't know what I was throwin' away."

Elaine didn't reply, and the lingering silence forced Jacob to look up again. He was surprised to find tears in her eyes.

He felt completely inept. "I'm sorry in more ways than I can say. I know I haven't treated you right, and I've blamed you for all sorts of things that you had nothing to do with. I've been short with the kids and even shorter with you."

"How can it work?"

"Maybe it won't," he replied honestly. "There's a heap of hurt to climb over. But maybe if we both try hard, we can do it."

In a whisper, her eyes downcast, she asked, "What about love?"

He'd lain awake most of last night, remembering things about Elaine, remembering those first days they were together in California, remembering their wedding, their honeymoon, their return to River Bluff. Somewhere in the midst of all those memories, he'd realized all the things he'd felt for her, back in the beginning. He'd cared about her enough to propose. He'd wanted to get married as much as she had, though he'd conveniently forgotten that over the years. Had it been love he'd felt for her? He couldn't say for sure. But it had been something.

"We'll work on loving each other," he said, hoping that would be enough. "We'll work on being a real family. What do you say, Elaine? Can we give it another go?"

~

Del paced the doctor's waiting room while his father-in-law, arms folded across his chest, observed from his chair near the window.

"What's taking so long?"

Frank replied, "He's just being thorough. Why don't you sit down, or he'll have to examine you next."

But Del knew he wouldn't be able to sit still. "I should have made her come see Dr. Carson. She hasn't been herself lately. No energy. No appetite. Just not herself."

"Yes, I've noticed. But I'm sure it's nothing but a cold or a touch of the flu."

"I hope you're—"

The door to the examination room opened, and Dr. Carson stepped into the waiting area, closing the door behind him. Del peered at the physician's face, looking for a clue. Was he frowning with concern? Was he troubled? Del couldn't tell.

"Doctor?" Del said, fear in his voice.

Dr. Carson shook his head slowly. "No need for alarm." His

gaze flicked to Frank, then back to Del. "Although I'd say your life won't be the same after today."

Del wasn't comforted by the doctor's words. "What are you saying? Is Miriam—"

"Your wife's expecting."

"Expecting?"

Frank came to stand beside him.

"A baby." The doctor grinned. "She's going to have a baby."

"But you said . . . but we thought . . . but I—"

Frank slapped him on the back. "Del, you're going to be a father. Praise the Lord! I'm going to be a grandpa!"

He looked at his father-in-law, then at the doctor. "A baby," he whispered. And finally the shock wore off and the joy overflowed. "We're gonna have a baby!"

The three men laughed and shook hands with exuberance for a minute or two more. Then Del asked if he could see his wife.

"Sure," the doctor replied. "She's waiting for you. Go on in."

~

Del's baby. I'm going to have Del's baby.

Miriam let the words replay over and over again in her mind, savoring them, yet not quite believing them. After all this time, after being told it was doubtful she could conceive, after trying so hard to accept with grace her childlessness, she was going to have a baby.

The door to the examination room opened, and Del stepped in. Beaming from ear to ear, he looked like a kid at the carnival.

Thank You, Jesus. Thank You for this moment.

Del crossed the room. "Hey, Mom."

"Hey, Pop."

"When's the day? I forgot to ask."

"Dr. Carson thinks around the middle of June."

Del lovingly stroked the side of her face, from temple to jaw, with the back of his fingertips.

"I feel a little silly," she said with a soft laugh. "I should've guessed. All the signs were there. But I never expected it would happen. After eleven years . . ." she let her voice trail away.

"Oh, we of little faith. We seem to have forgotten that our Lord is a Lord of miracles." He leaned over and kissed her on the lips, reverently. When the kiss ended, he kept his face near hers, and with a mischievous twinkle in his eyes, said, "Guess we're not such an old married couple, after all. Won't Sally be surprised."

They laughed together, feeling silly, giddy, young, and wildly happy. The future was bright, full of endless possibilities for them and their precious child.

CHAPTER TWENTY-ONE

MIRIAM DRIED HER HANDS ON A DISH TOWEL ON HER WAY TO answer the doorbell.

"Hi, Mrs. Tucker," Sally said from the other side of the screen door. "Happy Thanksgiving."

"Why, Sally. I wasn't expecting you."

"If it's a bad time, I can—"

"No. Don't be silly." She pushed the door open wide. "Come in out of the cold."

"Thanks."

"Would you like a cup of tea?" Miriam headed toward the kitchen. "I've got the kettle on."

"Sure." Sally followed her.

Miriam poured hot water over tea bags in two cups, then carried them to the small kitchen table.

"Is Mr. Tucker here?"

"Not at the moment. I discovered I'm short one place setting for dinner, so he went to the store. One advantage of running our own business, I guess. You can get what you need, even on a holiday. Did you need to see him?"

Sally shook her head. "Actually, it's you I wanted to talk to."

Miriam lifted an eyebrow as she sank onto the chair opposite the girl.

"There was so much excitement last week, what with you finding out about the baby and all, that I never found time to . . . to say thanks."

145

"For what?"

A blush rose up Sally's neck and spilled onto her cheeks. She stared into her teacup. "If it weren't for what you said to me . . . well, I think I might've gotten into . . . trouble with Hadley." She looked at Miriam again. "That Saturday, when we went to Boise, he . . . a . . . he got kind of fresh."

Alarmed, Miriam leaned forward, taking hold of Sally's hand atop the table. "What did he do?"

"Nothing really." She flushed hotter and glanced away. "But I . . . I had to get out of his car to make sure it didn't."

Miriam was too angry to speak.

"I guess he figured he'd done me a favor, taking me out, and it was time to pay up." Unshed tears welled in Sally's eyes. "But I remembered what you said, about how there's always conse-quences for the choices we make. I thought how what I want is to get married to a man who'll love me the way Mr. Tucker loves you, and I knew the price Hadley was asking was too high." She took a deep breath, then let it out on a sigh. "So I got out and started walking home. It was dark and kinda scary, but then Tad Farnsdale came along and gave me a ride the rest of the way to town."

"I'd like to take a strap to Hadley."

"Please don't tell anybody," Sally said quickly. "I feel like an idiot already. You can tell Mr. Tucker, I guess, but nobody else."

"Of course." Miriam shook her head while giving the girl's hand a squeeze. "I won't say a word to anyone else."

The girl leaned back in her chair. "Last Sunday, our pastor read a Scripture that I went and looked at later." She reached into her jacket pocket and withdrew a slip of paper. "I wrote it down. It says, 'You yourselves are our letter of recommendation, written on your hearts, to be known and read by all men.' I don't know why, but it made me think how others are always looking at us and reading us, like the Bible says there. Know what I mean?"

"I think so."

"Well, that's like me and you. I've learned from you 'cause I've been reading the way you live, the way you are with Mr. Tucker and him with you."

"That's rather profound, Sally."

She shrugged, but looked pleased at the same time. "Well, it just seems to me that I want others to read me and know that I'm living the way God wants. That I'm going to stay pure so I can have the kind of marriage He has planned for me. No boy's popular enough to give that up." She shrugged again, then rose from the chair. "I better get home and help Mom with the turkey or something. But I had to say thanks."

"I'm glad you shared with me." Miriam rose and followed Sally toward the front door.

Once there, Sally turned and embraced her, hugging tightly. "I love you, Mrs. Tucker. I'm real glad for you and Mr. Tucker and the baby and all."

Before Miriam could reply, the girl released her and left in a hurry.

Her heart warmed by the encounter, Miriam returned to the kitchen, dabbing at the corners of her eyes with her apron and sniffing softly. She couldn't wait for Del to get home so she could share what Sally had said.

A letter . . . to be known and read by all men.

She smiled, still teary eyed, as she began peeling the potatoes.

~

Standing in the stockroom at the back of the five-and-dime, Del stared at the shelves stacked with merchandise. He was certain he'd placed the boxes of dishware back here, but he couldn't seem to find them. Miriam wasn't going to be happy if he returned empty-handed. He thought it would be just as easy to call her father and ask him to bring the needed place setting from his house, but Miriam wouldn't hear of it. Especially since Frank was bringing Jim Hogan's widowed sister, Allison Keene, as his guest.

"A date!" Miriam had exclaimed to Del when she shared the news. "Dad's got a date!"

Thanksgiving at the Tucker home had to be perfect—right down to the place settings—because Frank Gresham was bringing a lady friend with him.

Not that Miriam should even be cooking Thanksgiving dinner this year, Del thought as he went after the stepladder. She should be resting. It was barely ten days since she'd passed out at church. They should have called Thanksgiving off.

Miriam insisted she was over the bad patch. Her appetite had improved a little, and she wasn't feeling nearly so tired. "I'm not calling off Thanksgiving dinner," she'd told Del. "I'm perfectly fine."

Del set the stepladder near the back shelves and began to climb.

He supposed Miriam should really stay home from the store. He could hire another part-time person, maybe a high school student like Sally. Might as well do it now. Miriam wouldn't be working once the baby came.

A burst of pleasure warmed his heart. A baby. His and Miriam's baby. After eleven years, they were finally going to have a child in their home.

Thank You, Father God, for this unexpected but most wanted blessing. You have blessed me, indeed.

He spied the box he was looking for. Bracing his left foot on the top of the ladder, he reached for the box. That was when his bad leg buckled. He felt himself pitching sideways, grabbed for something to hold on to but found only air. His temple struck a shelf, spinning him so that he hit the floor on his stomach. A split second later, his forehead slammed the concrete.

Miriam . . .

~

The hospital was quiet at four in the morning. Rounds would begin in a couple of hours, but for now, nurses sat at their station, going over charts, while patients slept. A pale light from the hall came through the half-open door, and a small reading lamp that her dad had brought from the store glowed softly on the bedside stand.

Miriam leaned forward, holding Del's limp hand between both of hers. *It's been five days, Lord. Please make him wake up. I don't think I can bear another day like this. God, I'm so tired.*

Her gaze shifted from Del to her father, who dozed in a chair in the corner. On Thanksgiving afternoon, Frank Gresham had followed the ambulance to Boise in his automobile and had scarcely left Miriam's side since. Others had made the drive into Boise as well. Sally and her mother, Pastor Desmond, Sheriff Jagger, even Patrick and Grace Finch.

Jacob had come, too. "Elaine and I are trying to work it out," he'd told Miriam. "You were right. About a lot of things. I just wanted you to know. And I'm here for you if I can help. As your friend. That's all. I'll understand if it's too late for that, but I wanted you to know."

An infinitesimal movement of Del's fingers between her hands drew her gaze to the bed. Del's eyes were open. He was looking at her.

"Del!" She kept her voice low, although she wanted to shout his name at the top of her lungs.

He made an effort to smile, then whispered hoarsely, "Hospital?"

"Yes."

"How long?"

"Five days." A lump formed in her throat. Tears welled, threatening to fall.

He nodded, closed his eyes, sighed.

"Dad's here with me." She stood and leaned closer. "Folks from River Bluff are all praying for you."

"Honey . . ." He opened his eyes. "I'm going home."

"Soon. As soon as you're better. The doctor says it will take time, but—"

"No, Miriam. I mean I'm going home."

Her heart hammered. She felt hot. She felt cold. Her knees were like rubber.

"I'll see you in heaven."

"Del," she whispered, "don't say that. I can't bear to lose you. I'll be so alone."

Another small smile, meant to encourage her, though it failed. "You won't be alone. Jesus never leaves you."

"You can't go." She tightened her grip on his hand. "You have to be here for our baby. Remember the baby, Del?"

"That's a miracle, you know. God gave me just enough time, didn't He?"

"I can't raise the baby without you." Tears streamed down her face, falling onto the sheets. "How can I raise him without you?"

His voice seemed softer, farther away. "The same way as if I were here. You'll raise him with love. In the truth of Christ." He found the strength to lift his hand and touch her damp cheek. "You're going to be fine, Miriam. So will our child. Have faith, my love."

"Del, don't. O God . . . O Jesus . . ."

His eyes drifted closed once again. For the longest while—

an eternity, it seemed—she heard only the faint sound of his shallow breathing.

Finally, he smiled. A real smile this time, one that came without effort. A smile that caused his entire face to glow with an inner warmth.

"It's You," he said softly, joy apparent in those two simple words.

Then Del Tucker went home.

JULIANNA

SUMMER 2001

CHAPTER TWENTY-TWO

"HE *DIED?*" I SAID, MY GAZE MOVING FROM SALLY FARNSDALE TO Jacob McAllister.

The old man nodded.

"But that's so unfair."

"What makes you think life's supposed to be fair?" Jacob asked, his voice gentle rather than condemning.

I was angry. Angry for Miriam. I shouldn't have been, of course. I'd never known her, never even heard of her before today. And yet—

I considered leaving, right then and there. These people with all their God talk made me uncomfortable. Yet I couldn't leave. Not before I heard the rest of Miriam Tucker's story.

Sally trailed her fingertip around the lip of the soda glass, drawing my gaze to her.

Softly, as if speaking to herself rather than to the rest of us in the room, she said, "Miriam claimed that year was the hardest of all her life. Even harder than the trials that came later on." She glanced at me. "She also said it was the year she grew closest to God—she either had to depend solely upon Him, cling tighter to Jesus, or she had to reject Him completely. And she couldn't do the latter."

What if Leland were to die? What would I cling to?

Those questions disturbed me. It surprised me, knowing with a sudden certainty that if my husband died, I would have

. . . nothing. It seemed I could see a vast abyss before me and no way to cross it.

I pushed the unpleasant thought from my mind. "Did Miriam have the baby all right?"

"Yes." Sally returned the glass to the box. "A boy. Luke. How we celebrated his arrival. Didn't we, Jacob?"

"We sure did. That was Miriam's last summer in River Bluff, too." He looked at me. "She closed the store after Del died. I'm not sure she set foot in it ever again. Then, when little Luke was about three months old, she moved to Boise. Between Del's insurance policies and the sale of her house and business, she was pretty set. She wasn't rich by any means, but she was comfortable. Smart, too. Invested wisely over the years." He waved his hand. "She bought this house that fall and lived here right up to the day she died."

"Oh, look at these," Sally interrupted. She held out the gold earrings I'd seen earlier. "Do you know the story behind these, Jacob? I don't think I ever saw them before."

"I know the story. Back in the early sixties, that was. My goodness. I think we were doing the twist and preparing for the British invasion of the Beatles." He chuckled. "What a different time it was."

MIRIAM

SPRING 1963

CHAPTER TWENTY-THREE

"Luke!" Miriam dropped her purse and car keys on the entry-hall table. "Dad!" She glanced in the oval mirror above the table while removing her pillbox hat. "Where are you two?"

No answer.

She made her way toward the rear of the house, not stopping until she reached the door—which, she wasn't surprised to find, had been left wide open.

"How many times do I have to tell them?" she muttered.

But she wasn't truly irritated with her father or son. Why bother? Both of them knew how to charm her out of a bad mood.

She leaned against the jamb and stared at the large, sloping backyard, bordered by tall shade trees and carefully tended flower gardens. At the far end of the yard were Frank and Luke, throwing a baseball back and forth.

Nothing like a beautiful spring day to bring out the ball and glove.

She pushed open the screen. "Hey, where's my welcome?"

"Mom!" Luke dropped his mitt and raced toward her, looking as if he hadn't seen her in a week instead of a few hours.

It made her feel like a million bucks.

She stepped onto the stoop. "Hi, honey."

"Grandpa's showing me how to throw a curveball."

"Good for Grandpa." She ruffled Luke's hair. "How about your schoolwork? Did you get it done?"

"Ah, Mom. It's a *Saturday*."

Her dad arrived at the bottom of the steps. "It's my fault, pixie. I wanted some exercise."

"Oh, Dad, please." She rolled her eyes. No forty-one-year-old woman should be referred to as "pixie," but breaking Frank Gresham of the habit seemed hopeless. So she turned her attention back to her son. "Luke, you heard me. Up to your room right now, and do your math papers."

The boy shot his grandpa a look, seeking an ally.

"Mind your mom. We'll work on that curveball after church tomorrow."

Luke groaned dramatically as he went into the house.

Miriam smiled. "He's quite the athlete, isn't he?"

"That he is."

"Like Del."

"Yes, he's a lot like Del. He's a good boy. You've done a fine job raising him."

"No small thanks to you." She turned and reentered the house.

"How was the luncheon?"

"Boring." She took the casserole dish containing that night's supper from the refrigerator and set it in the cold oven, then turned the temperature control to three-fifty. "Just once I wish they'd get a speaker under the age of ninety."

Frank chuckled. "Can't be as bad as all that."

"Almost." Miriam sank onto a chair at the table and kicked off her patent-leather pumps.

"Bert Rey stopped by earlier," her dad said as he sat opposite her. "He brought some brochures about that camp. Luke says he wants to go."

"Isn't he still a bit young to go for a whole week?" She swept her hair away from her face. "He isn't even ten yet."

"Is it Luke's age or just that you'd miss him too much?"

She met his gaze. "Guilty as charged."

"Pixie?" He leaned across the table, placing an age-wrinkled hand over hers. "Sometimes I worry you're letting life pass you by. Bert's getting serious, you know."

"I know."

"He's a good man."

"I know that, too."

"But?"

She shrugged. "Nothing really. I like Bert." She slipped her hand from her father's and rose from the chair. "I need to get out of this dress and into something comfortable."

"And I'd better get on my way home. Allison's got a bridge party at our house tonight, and she'll be madder'n all get-out if I'm late getting back." He stood, walked around the table, and gave Miriam a kiss on the cheek. "See you at church."

She walked with him toward the front door. "Thanks for staying with Luke this afternoon, Dad. He really loves spending time with you." Softly, so her voice wouldn't carry up the stairs, she added, "I nearly forgot to tell you. I bought that camera he wants. Now I can hardly wait for his birthday to give it to him."

"You've always hated to wait," Frank replied with a wink and a smile. "For anything." He gave her another peck on the cheek, then headed out the door and down the steps.

Miriam watched him go, thinking how right he was. Impatience had always been one of her faults.

When Frank reached his Nash, he waved at her before getting into the automobile. She waved back, then closed the door and went upstairs. On her way, she peeked inside Luke's room. He was obediently bent over the homework papers on his desk, his back toward her, so she continued on without saying a word.

Sunshine filtered through the sheer, mauve-colored draperies, giving her bedroom a rosy glow. From the floral bedspread to the frilly skirt around the dressing table to the delicate nicknacks on the bedside table, everything proclaimed that the room belonged to a woman. A woman without a man.

"Sometimes I worry you're letting life pass you by."

She frowned. Was her dad right? Was she letting life pass her by?

Her thoughts churning, Miriam opened the closet door, then unzipped her dress and stepped out of it. The first year after Del's death had been a hard one. She'd spent most of her pregnancy in tears. Every holiday had served to remind her that she couldn't celebrate it with the husband she loved. Other families in River Bluff were constant reminders that her precious son would grow up without his father.

Moving to Boise had helped, and decorating her new home—an older house that had fallen into disrepair—had filled many of her lonely hours. She'd taken her time with the wallpapering, painting, refinishing, and buying furniture. She'd wanted to put her personal stamp on every single room, and she'd succeeded. And while she'd worked on the house, God had worked on healing her heart.

"Bert's getting serious, you know."

"Yes, Dad," she whispered. "I know."

Bert Rey was Luke's Cub Scout leader. A divorced father with a son of his own to raise, he and Miriam had become acquainted at the start of the school year. They attended the same church and had several mutual friends. It was easy to like Bert. He was thoughtful, funny, interesting, and had a wonderful smile. No, he wasn't the most handsome man in the world. He was like a teddy bear, round and cuddly, which Miriam found appealing.

And yet . . .

She closed her closet door, then finished buttoning her blouse while crossing to the bedroom window.

"And yet he isn't Del?" She tried the words aloud, wondering if it was the reason she didn't allow something more serious to develop with Bert.

She looked down at the vegetable garden, lying fallow at the end of April, awaiting the spring planting. "Am I lying fallow, Lord? Is that what You're trying to tell me?"

Her dad seemed to think so.

Of course, Frank Gresham was also a happily married man. After three years of a long-distance courtship, he'd proposed to Jim Hogan's sister, Allison Keene, and she'd accepted. They'd wed two weeks later. Shortly afterward, at the age of sixty, Frank had decided to retire. He'd sold the drugstore, and he and Allison had moved to Boise, where they could be nearer his daughter and grandson. For the past seven years, the Greshams had lived a short six blocks from Miriam and Luke, and Luke adored having his granddad nearby.

But, Miriam wondered now, did Luke need a man, in addition to his granddad, in the home? Did he need a stepfather? Someone like Bert?

"Hey, Mom!"

Pulled from her musings, she turned. "What?"

"I need your help with this math stuff."

She smiled. "Coming, honey."

Miriam's life didn't seem fallow at the moment.

CHAPTER TWENTY-FOUR

Yanking off her gardening gloves on the run, Miriam reached the phone on the fifth ring. "Hello?"

"Hello," said a male voice. "Is this Miriam Tucker?"

"Yes. Who's calling, please."

"It's Jacob."

She paused a moment before asking, "McAllister?"

"In the flesh."

"My goodness, Jacob. It's been ages since I heard your voice."

"Nine years, to be exact."

"It's such a surprise. How are you? Are you calling from San Francisco?"

"No. I'm in Boise. We're moving back to Idaho."

"To River Bluff?"

"Nothing for us to go back to there now that my dad's gone and my brothers have all moved away. No, we're moving to Boise. I'm going to open my own insurance agency here. Just closed the deal on an office near downtown today. Tomorrow I've gotta find us a house to rent until we're ready to buy."

Miriam settled onto a kitchen stool near the wall phone. "How's Elaine? And the kids?"

"Fine. Everybody's fine." He chuckled. "I don't suppose you heard we've got another set of twins."

"No! Really?"

"A boy and a girl this time. Rachel and Bobby. They're almost two."

She smiled. "You sound happy, Jacob."

"You better believe it." His voice turned more serious. "In lots of ways, I've got you to thank for it."

Miriam didn't know how to respond.

After a few moments of silence, Jacob said, "I'm not sayin' it was easy. Even when we moved back to California, the way Elaine wanted, I had my doubts we could save our marriage. There was a load of hurt and pain we were both packin' around. You know as well as anybody that it was mostly my fault. Elaine deserves the credit for stickin' it out. She had plenty of reasons not to."

Miriam continued to listen in silence.

"The story's too long to go into now. Suffice it to say, I quit drinking and started loving my wife and kids the way a man's supposed to."

"I'm glad for you, Jacob. Very glad."

"Listen, I'd love for us all to get together once the family's settled in. Be good to catch up on old times."

"I'd like that too."

"Well then, when Elaine and the kids get up here, we'll give you a call. I'm dyin' to see Luke. He was only a couple months old last time I saw him. And how 'bout your dad? I heard through the grapevine he got married and is living in Boise."

"Yes, about seven years ago."

"Hard to imagine." He paused, then asked, "How about you? Anyone special in your life?"

Why did it seem as if *everybody* was asking her that question lately?

She surprised herself by answering, "There might be."

"Glad to hear it. I hope to meet him. I guess I'd better hang up now. Good talking to you, Miriam."

"You, too, Jacob."

"Bye."

"Good-bye. Have a safe move."

~

The Webelos Scout Pack #442 met on Thursday afternoons in the fellowship hall of the New Morning Christian Center. The meeting place had changed this year, but Bert Rey had been a cubmaster ever since his son, Andy, joined the Tiger Cubs in first grade.

In the beginning, Bert's wife, Cheryl—make that his *ex-*wife—had been an active participant, but she'd left Bert and Andy three years ago. Left town without a trace. It wasn't until she was gone that he'd learned of her long-standing affair with another man. Not the man she'd run off with, however. That guy was someone new. Someone younger and richer.

Last year Bert had received divorce papers from out of the country. With the dissolution of their marriage, Cheryl had given sole custody of their son to Bert. She'd made it clear in the accompanying documents that she had no desire to see Andy again. It was as if the boy didn't exist to her.

Bert had hated Cheryl for that, even more than for leaving him. Maybe he still hated her for it sometimes. But he tried not to dwell on it anymore.

"Don't forget to ask your parents about camp," he called to the departing scouts. "We need definite numbers of those going in a couple of weeks."

He gathered books and supplies and dropped them into a cardboard box.

"Look, Mom," Luke Tucker said excitedly. "I earned my new badge."

Bert turned in time to see Miriam kneel down and hug her son.

"Honey, that's terrific. I'm so proud of you." She glanced over Luke's head, her gaze meeting Bert's. She smiled. "But I knew you would. You always give a hundred percent." She stood again.

Bert walked toward her, returning her smile. "I thought I was supposed to drop Luke at your house today," he said.

"You were." She shrugged. "But I needed a break from yard work, and it was a beautiful day for a walk."

Miriam was what was beautiful, he thought, even with grass stains on the knees of her capri pants and a smudge of dirt on the tip of her chin.

Bert's relationship with Miriam was still somewhat tentative after six dates in a third as many months. She'd become his sister in Christ first, then a trusted confidante—another single parent who understood the ups and downs of raising a son—and maybe, she'd become his "lady friend," as one of the guys in the church men's group put it.

"Get your things, honey," Miriam told Luke, her voice intruding on Bert's thoughts. The boy hurried off to obey.

As soon as Luke was out of earshot, Bert asked, "Have you given more thought to Luke's going to camp? We've gotta know by next week. Have you decided?"

She nodded, then shook her head, then shrugged.

He raised an eyebrow.

Miriam laughed softly. "Yes, I've thought about it. No, I haven't decided. I just keep thinking he's terribly young to go away for a whole week. He isn't even ten yet."

"He's the same age as all the boys who are going."

"I know, but—"

"Mind a bit of advice?" He knew he was treading on dangerous ground now, but he decided to forge ahead. "Don't mollycoddle him, Miriam. You won't be doing him any favors by it."

All traces of laughter disappeared from her expression.

"Look," Bert blundered on, figuring it was too late to back out now, "I know Luke. I've been his cubmaster all year. He's a good kid. He's athletic and smart. Never reckless the way some boys are. He'd excel at camp, and I think you know it. Turn him loose a little, Miriam. Sometimes you hang on way too tight."

She looked across the fellowship hall to where her son stood talking with Andy and a couple of other boys.

I've really blown it with her now.

But Miriam surprised him. "You could be right, Bert. Maybe I am being overprotective." She met his gaze again. "I'll let him go to scout camp, but only because you're going to be there, too."

Her trust felt good. He was determined not to let her down.

CHAPTER TWENTY-FIVE

DESPITE ITS BEING MID-MAY, THERE WAS PLENTY OF SNOW LEFT IN the higher elevations. It sparkled on rocky mountaintops, and it peeked out from shadowy ravines. But Highway 21 was clear, and the sun reigned in a pristine blue sky that Saturday morning as the gray-and-black Ford Fairlane drove north toward Idaho City.

In the rear seat, Luke and Andy debated who was the best ballplayer in the major leagues. Pitcher Sandy Koufax seemed to have the edge, but the base-stealing Maury Morning Wills was a close second in the boys' opinion. In the front seat, Miriam and Bert sang along with the radio like a couple of teenagers, belting out, "Only love can break a heart," as if they knew what they were doing. Gene Pitney would've been proud.

They arrived at the hot springs resort in high spirits. With suits and towels in their arms, they scrambled out of the car, accompanied by their own laughter. After paying the fee, Bert and the boys headed for the men's locker room and Miriam for the women's.

Miriam smiled to herself as she changed from her shorts and cotton top into a one-piece swimming suit. She hadn't enjoyed herself this much in a long, long while.

Strange, she thought, the difference a couple of weeks could make.

She stepped into the shower stall and turned the lever. The spray that came through the nozzle was as cold as melted snow.

She shrieked in surprise and jumped out. Shivering, she hurried from the dressing room, tossed her towel onto a bench, and jumped into the pool's wonderfully warm water. When she came up for air, she heard her son's voice and used her arms to turn a hundred and eighty degrees.

Bert and the boys were engaged in an enthusiastic game of water basketball in the shallow end.

Bert and the boys . . .

She mulled those words over in her mind.

Bert and the boys . . .

It sounded almost like a family.

Is it what You want for me, God? I'm not sure I trust my heart when it comes to this.

Bert grabbed Andy and catapulted him toward Miriam. He flew through the air, landing with a great splash, drenching her face and hair.

"Get him!" Andy cried the instant he resurfaced, revengeful laughter in his voice.

Miriam let go of her questions and joined in the attack.

~

On two large plaid blankets spread on the gently sloped hillside, they ate their picnic lunch of fried chicken, potato salad, baked beans, and corn bread. Miriam's prizewinning spice cake was served for dessert, after which the boys pleaded to explore the nearby forest.

Bert listed a number of rules to be followed, then glanced at Miriam for her concurrence.

"Don't mollycoddle him." She could almost hear Bert repeating those words to her as she reluctantly nodded her approval.

"Okay," Bert continued, "look at your watch, Andy. What time is it?"

"Almost one-thirty."

"We want you back here at two o'clock. Understood?"

"Yes, Dad."

"And you're to stay together and within shouting distance of us. Agreed?"

"Yes."

"Luke?" Bert looked his way.

"Yes, sir. Thanks, Mom."

She hid her uncertainty behind a smile. "Have fun, and remember what Mr. Rey told you."

"We will."

The two boys raced up the hillside, leaping over a rotting log like a pair of young bucks.

"Relax, Miriam. They'll remember the rules. They're good Scouts."

She glanced at Bert, then started to clear away the food, putting leftovers into the cooler and picnic basket, tossing paper plates into a sack to throw away. Bert pitched in to help, and it wasn't long before they were finished.

"Miriam," Bert said when she started to gather up the blankets to carry to the car. "Do me a favor."

"What?" she replied distractedly.

"Leave the blankets where they are. Lie down on your back and stare up at the sky."

She looked at him.

He patted the spot beside him. "Right here, if you don't mind."

Nerves and anticipation shivered through her. "Why?"

"Because I asked you to. Is that enough reason?"

After a moment, she did his bidding.

Bert lay back, too. "Pretty, isn't it?"

He was right. It *was* pretty. Wisps of clouds floated against the blue. A ponderosa pine swayed gently, casting dancing shadows across her face—sun and shade, sun and shade, sun and shade. A hawk soared effortlessly above, wings outstretched.

Bert rolled onto his elbow, bringing his chest against her shoulder and his face into view. "Miriam . . ."

Her heart started banging like a kettledrum.

"Today's been fun."

Her gaze locked with his.

"I think maybe there could be something more between you and me. If we let it happen."

She swallowed.

He drew closer. "I'm going to kiss you, Miriam Tucker."

She nodded, granting permission.

It had been a good, long while since Miriam was kissed by a man in this particular manner. She felt more like an untried schoolgirl than a forty-one-year-old widow, uncertain which way to turn her head, where to put her hands, whether or not to close her eyes. She was keenly aware of the warm pressure of Bert's mouth upon hers, the scratchy stubble on his jaw, the pool-chlorine scent on his skin. But when all was said and done, she found the kiss . . . pleasant . . . and she wasn't sorry she'd allowed it to happen.

Bert drew back, his gaze searching hers. Her reaction must have satisfied him, for he smiled. "I have something for you." He sat up.

Miriam did the same.

Bert reached into his shirt pocket and withdrew some folded blue tissue paper. He held it toward her. "Sorry it isn't a fancier package."

"You really shouldn't—"

"Just take it, Miriam. Please."

She felt so ridiculously shy. Silly, but true. She accepted the small package, placed it in her lap, then unfolded the paper. In the center, she found a pair of earrings. They were gold, delicate, feminine, and exactly what she would have chosen for herself.

He cleared his throat. "I've been thinking. We're not kids, you and I. We're both raising our sons alone. We know what it means to be married, to share a life with someone else. We're believers, and I imagine we both know what we'd want in a spouse." He leaned toward her. "I'd like us to think seriously about making more of this thing between us—" he flicked his hand toward her, toward himself, back to her again—"than just friendship. I'd like us to see if we aren't meant to get . . . married."

She'd suspected, of course, what he was going to say. Still, hearing it out loud took her by surprise. "Married?"

"You must have thought about it at some time or another."

She thought of the difficulties of managing a home all alone—the broken dryer, the bad latch on the screen, the leaky faucet in the upstairs bathroom. She thought of the times Luke had been sick in the middle of the night and the comfort it would have been to have someone with her then. She thought of those moments when she'd seen a spectacular sunset and wanted to share it, only she was alone.

"Well, I suppose . . ." She let her voice trail away.

Bert took hold of her hand. "This isn't a proposal just yet. But maybe talking about marriage will help us discover if that's what's in our future."

"It makes sense," she replied softly.

"Good." He kissed her on the cheek, then rose to his feet and grabbed the cooler in one hand, the picnic basket in the other. "Here come the boys. Guess it's time to head back to town."

～

That night, Miriam had a hard time falling to sleep. She lay in her bed, at times praying, at others mulling over the years.

Would I want to get married again?

She wasn't sure.

What's Your will in this, Father?

The Bible said it was better to marry than to lust, but lust hadn't been one of her particular failings in the years since she lost her husband. She had plenty other sins to take its place, of course, but not lust. She believed marriage was an honorable estate, ordained by God. He'd created man and woman and made them one.

She rose from the bed and walked to the window, pushing aside the sheer drapes to stare at the moon-bathed yard. The garden no longer lay fallow as it had a couple of weeks before. She'd been tilling and hoeing, planting and watering all this past week.

Is there planting to do in me, Lord, in this season of my life?

If she considered marriage, what would that mean for Luke? Miriam had seen stepfamily situations that didn't work. Bert was fond of Luke now, but how would it be if the two boys were living in the same house? What if there was an argument, as there would most assuredly be? Whose side would Bert take? The side of right or the side of his own son, right or not?

Her dad thought she should get married. He believed her life would be better with a man, with a whole family. He'd certainly found happiness in a new marriage. Yet Miriam suspected he still missed her mother sometimes, even though he was blissfully content with Allison. He and Allison fit together in countless ways, as if they'd been married a lifetime.

"Would it be like that for Bert and me? Could I learn to love him?" She looked up at the starry sky. "Lord, I need to know what You want for us."

CHAPTER TWENTY-SIX

It was a balmy evening, that Friday at the end of May, the perfect kind of evening for a gathering of friends. In preparation for the get-together, Miriam and Luke had strung lights from house to tree limbs to telephone pole, giving the backyard a festive feeling that had grown more so when twilight arrived.

Standing in the back doorway, her shoulder leaning against the jamb, her arms folded across her chest, Miriam perused the scene before her, bits and pieces of conversations carried to her on the evening breeze.

Near the barbecue grill, the men discussed the successful orbiting of Earth by Major Gordon Cooper Jr. in the Mercury capsule *Faith 7*. Beneath the patio awning, the women debated whether or not *Lawrence of Arabia* deserved the Academy Award for best picture over *To Kill a Mockingbird* or *The Miracle Worker*. And on the lower section of lawn, the children played croquet, the rules strictly enforced by the sixteen-year-old McAllister twins, Valerie and Victoria.

Miriam felt contentment wash over her, a sense of well-being, of rightness with her world.

At that moment, Jacob broke away from the other men—Bert Rey, Frank Gresham, Charlie Ireland from church, and her neighbor Sam Watkins—and walked toward the house. She smiled, thinking that it was good to have her old friend back.

"Great party, Miriam," he said when he reached the back stoop. "Thanks for including me and the family."

"I'm glad you could come." She moved out of the doorway and sank onto the top step, hugging her knees with her arms.

Jacob joined her. "Luke's one terrific kid. You've gotta be proud."

She nodded, her gaze shifting toward the croquet game.

"Who'd've thought it?" Jacob said with a soft chuckle.

"Thought what?"

"That this is where we'd be."

She looked at him.

"You know. You and me, middle-aged, kids, mortgages. Just living ordinary lives."

"I like my ordinary life."

He grinned. "Me too." He chuckled again. "But when I think back to when we were kids, you wanting to be a famous movie star and me . . . well, who knows what I wanted? Anything other than to take that job with Tucker's Insurance. I hated the idea of being an insurance salesman. But you know what? I'm good at it. Really good."

"I know." It was her turn to laugh. "Del swore you could sell ice to an Eskimo."

"Did he?" He sounded both surprised and pleased at the compliment.

Laughter erupted from the group of men, drawing Miriam's and Jacob's gazes. Miriam's settled on Bert, who stood at the grill, flipping burgers with one hand and drinking soda from a can with the other.

"He seems a good sort," Jacob said. "I like him."

"Me too."

"Has he asked you to marry him?"

"Not exactly."

"What does that mean, 'not exactly'?"

"We've talked about the possibility of it in the future. What we need to know now is if it's God's will for us."

"How does anybody know something like that?"

She looked at him, unable to hide her surprise. "Because He'll tell us, of course."

Whatever Jacob might have said next was interrupted by Bert's loud announcement that the burgers were ready. "Grab your plates and come and get it!"

Nobody had to be told twice.

~

Jacob turned off the TV at the close of the news broadcast and looked toward his wife, lying beside him in bed, her head and shoulders propped up with pillows as she read a paperback novel.

"Did you enjoy yourself tonight?" he asked.

"What?" Elaine closed her book.

"Did you enjoy yourself tonight? I thought it was a nice group of people."

"Yes, I had a good time. Everyone was very friendly, Miriam especially. And Rose Ireland asked me to play golf with her next week."

"You should do it." He slid closer to his wife and placed his arm behind her shoulders. "I was thinking, maybe we could visit that church they all go to. It's not far from our new place, and it would probably be good for the kids, help them make friends over the summer."

She placed her head on his chest. "It might be good for you and me, too."

"Yeah, I know."

Jacob reached over Elaine and turned out the light, then edged back into place, his wife still nestled in his arms. It wasn't long before he knew she'd fallen asleep, her breathing slow and rhythmic. But slumber escaped him.

He kept thinking about Miriam, about what she'd said tonight, about knowing God's will because God would tell her. She'd said it with such complete certainty, as if it were as ordinary an event as picking up the phone and calling her neighbor.

Back in River Bluff, the McAllister family had been a churchgoing one, like the Greshams. Jacob had memorized his Bible verses right alongside Miriam when they were in grade school. He'd eaten plenty of meals at the various socials and even been to a revival meeting or two in his youth. He believed in the things he'd learned while growing up, things like God creating the heavens and earth and Jesus' birth and death on the cross.

And yet Miriam's comment tonight had caused him to see that she had . . . oh, he didn't know . . . something beyond mere belief. It wasn't that she'd "got religion," as he'd once put it. It was something that went deeper.

He thought back to the time right before and after Del Tucker died, and he realized he'd seen the same thing in her then. Despite her grief, there'd been something stronger that carried her through. Something Jacob didn't have.

Jacob had given up booze years ago, after seeing what it was doing to him. He and Elaine had somehow managed to salvage a doomed marriage and learned to love each other. Jacob enjoyed his work and was able to provide well for his family. Elaine made a good home for them and was a terrific mother. Their kids were healthy and thriving.

Jacob was living the American dream. He had it all.

Or at least, he'd thought so.

But tonight, as he'd listened to Miriam, as he'd witnessed the expression on her face, he felt a strange hunger in his heart, and he knew he wanted . . . something more.

"Maybe you're using God as an excuse."

She met his gaze, answering with certainty. "No, I'm not."

Bert got up, paced away from the bench to a nearby tree, turned and looked at her. "I love you, Miriam. I do. Since you came into my life, I've been a different man. You gave me hope. We'd be good together, you and I. Our sons would have both a mom and a dad. We'd make a strong family unit. I think you know that."

She nodded.

"You care about me. Maybe you even love me. If you'd give us a little more time—"

"Time won't make the difference, Bert," she interrupted gently. "I have to do what I know the Lord wants." She rose from the bench. "I think I'd better go." As she turned, she added, "I'm sorry. So very sorry."

She walked home, mentally replaying everything she'd said. A flicker of uncertainty caused her to wonder if she'd done the right thing. She was fond of Bert. She might have learned to love him, given more time. They could have had a good marriage. She wouldn't have to be alone any longer. Was it possible she—?

Abruptly, she pushed away the doubts.

She'd learned over the years to recognize the voice of God when He spoke to her. She'd also learned that obedience now was better than repentance later. She knew without question the Lord had told her there would be times of affliction in her future, but He had also promised to go with her.

Jesus is my Husband, my Savior, my Beloved. I'm not alone.

Peace washed over her, a peace beyond understanding.

JULIANNA

SUMMER 2001

CHAPTER TWENTY-SEVEN

Jacob's voice drifted into silence, and after a moment or two, he rose to his feet and shuffled to the window. His expression was pensive as he stared through the glass.

I was thoughtful, too. I was considering the many losses Miriam had experienced before she'd reached my age.

My life, in comparison, had been one of ease. I was almost ashamed to admit how easy. My parents and grandparents were all living and in good health. My daughter had caused me no more than the usual stress associated with the teen years, raging female hormones, and pulling away from her mother's apron strings. Leland was a good provider, even if his work did force him to keep long hours. We had a lovely home in an upscale neighborhood, two new cars, and a boat for those rare times when we escaped to our cabin by the lake.

Jacob and Sally had both spoken of Miriam's faith as if it were the most natural thing in the world, about how it had strengthened her and brought her through the dark times. But what kind of God demanded that a woman raise her child alone and warned her there were even more troubles to come? It seemed extremely unfair.

Jacob McAllister had asked me why I believed life was supposed to be fair.

Well, didn't everyone think so?

Apparently not these two. Apparently not Miriam.

That bothered me. What had Miriam Tucker had that I didn't?

"What happened to Bert?" I asked, uncomfortable with the lingering silence and my own thoughts.

It was the young woman named Christy who answered me. "He met a really terrific lady and got married a couple years later. He was always saying how God turned things to good, just like He promised."

Sean, the middle-aged gentleman of the group who'd said little up to now, leaned forward and took an item from the box. I couldn't see what it was.

"This is about the time I came along," he said softly, as if to himself. Then he held up the 1972 campaign button.

"Was Miriam a big Nixon supporter?" I asked.

"That wasn't why she saved it." Jacob turned from the window. "She kept it 'cause it symbolized the times. Everything changed so fast. All the absolutes we grew up with disappeared overnight. The patriotism everyone felt during World War II was forgotten. Soldiers serving their country became the enemy, even those not in Vietnam."

I nodded, pretending I remembered more than I did. I hadn't cared about anything back then except ridding my face of new zits and whether or not the cutest boy on the junior high football team would invite me to the school dance.

Sally took the button from Sean. "I suppose every generation predicts the end of civilization because of the antics of the young. It's certainly how most adults felt about those years."

"Seemed like the whole world was coming apart at the seams," Jacob continued. "The Mai Lay massacre, *Apollo 13*, Watergate, Kent State, the invasion of Cambodia. The economy was bad and unemployment was high."

"Free love," Sally added, her voice low. "Free love that cost too much."

Jacob returned to his chair. "LSD and marijuana."

Sally pressed the campaign button into Jacob's hand, then folded his fingers over it and squeezed gently. "Thank God our kids came through okay, even if it was a bumpy ride."

"I sometimes wondered if there was more I could've done for Luke," Jacob said softly. "If only I could've done more, maybe things would've been different for him and Miriam. Maybe . . ."

MIRIAM

WINTER 1971

CHAPTER TWENTY-EIGHT

MIRIAM HEARD THE SCREAM OF THE ELECTRIC GUITAR THE MOMENT she opened her car door.

Is there anyone in the neighborhood who can't *hear it?*

Anger flared to life, dissipating the remnants of peace and joy she'd felt upon leaving the Sunday evening service. She grabbed her Bible and purse off the seat, then got out of the car and marched toward the house.

"Luke!" she shouted the instant she was inside. "Luke, stop that racket this instant!"

Another shrill twang was his only reply. The noise set her teeth on edge. She dropped everything onto the entry table, shed her coat and draped it over a chair, then hurried up the staircase.

"Lucas Delaney Tucker!" she cried as she burst into his room.

Sitting in the middle of the bed, sliding his left hand along the neck of the guitar while creating an earthshaking cacophony with the pick held between right finger and thumb, Luke opened his eyes and gave her a blank stare.

Miriam strode to the electrical outlet and yanked the plug from the wall.

The silence was deafening.

She turned toward the bed. "What on earth were you thinking? It's a Sunday evening. It's a wonder the neighbors didn't call the police."

"I've got a right to make music in my own house, don't I?"

"*That* was not music."

Color rose from his neck into his cheeks. "Chill out, Mom."

Who is he?

The boy on the bed was supposed to be her son, but Miriam didn't recognize him. Not anymore. This seventeen-year-old male was sullen and moody. His hair needed a good washing, not to mention a trim. His clothes looked as if he'd lived in them for the past week.

Keeping her voice as level as possible, she said, "Don't you speak to me like that, Luke. You're under eighteen and you live in my home. As long as that's true, you'll show respect for your mother the way you were taught."

"So you're gonna keep hassling me 'til I'm outta here, right?"

Anger surged again, and Miriam feared she would say something she shouldn't. Retreat seemed a better option. "Get to bed. Tomorrow's a school day." She dropped the guitar's electrical cord and walked toward the door. "Good night," she added before passing into the hallway.

Luke didn't reply.

O Lord, help me. I'm at my wit's end.

She stepped into her bedroom and closed the door. Crossing to her bed, she fell onto it, burying her face in a pillow while fighting tears.

I feel eighty-nine instead of forty-nine. I need Your strength to see me through. I'm so . . . so alone.

Miriam felt guilty for admitting it. The Lord had been her best friend, her provider, her ever-present help. Above all, He'd been the husband He'd promised He would be. But right now she wished she could curl up in someone's arms and cry. She wanted arms around her that she could feel.

I'm sorry, Lord, but it's true. Luke's driving me crazy. I don't

*know what to say to him. Where's the boy who liked going to church?
Where's the boy who liked helping me in the house and yard? I knew
things would change when he became a teen. I didn't expect to keep
him tied to my apron strings. I was prepared to let him grow up and
away. But this isn't what I expected. Sometimes I think he hates me.*

Miriam rolled onto her back and stared at the ceiling.

*How do I reach him, Jesus? If it were only long hair and dreadful
music, I could deal with it, but I'm afraid it's something more. I'm
frightened.*

TRUST ME, BELOVED.

I'm trying.

The bedside clock ticked away the seconds. A winter's wind
brushed tree branches against the side of the house.

Miriam closed her eyes and listened.

DO NOT FEAR, FOR I HAVE REDEEMED YOU; I HAVE CALLED
YOU BY NAME; YOU ARE MINE!

"Yes, Lord."

I WILL BRING YOUR OFFSPRING FROM THE EAST, AND GATHER
YOU FROM THE WEST.

She sat up and reached for her Bible on the nightstand. She
flipped the pages until she reached Isaiah, the forty-third chapter. She read the fifth verse aloud: "'Do not fear, for I am with
you; I will bring your offspring from the east, and gather you
from the west.'"

GIVE LUKE TO ME, BELOVED.

Miriam hesitated a heartbeat before responding. *Okay, Lord.
I gave him to You when he was born. Now I'll give him to You again.*

~

Miriam awakened at four o'clock in the morning. She tossed and
turned for a while, but when it was obvious she wasn't going
back to sleep, she arose. She grabbed her bathrobe, put on her

slippers, then went downstairs. After brewing coffee and pouring herself a cup, she entered her studio, settling into her favorite chair.

Not long after she'd stopped seeing Bert back in '63, Miriam had taken an art class. She'd thought it would fill some of the empty hours. She hadn't guessed how much she would love working with oils and watercolors. Certainly she hadn't expected she would have any talent for it. But she did.

At first she'd painted only for her own pleasure. Then she'd given in to the badgering of her friends and allowed Rose Ireland to hang one of her landscapes in the Irelands' gift shop.

And it *sold!*

Five years after that first sale, Miriam had a small but loyal following of collectors. She'd recently completed a portrait of the governor that was now prominently displayed in the capitol building. What a lot of hoopla her friends had made about that!

As she sipped coffee, Miriam's gaze drifted around the room until it reached her latest endeavor. A portrait of Del.

How different life might have been if he hadn't died so young.

She rose from her chair and crossed the studio to study the canvas. It seemed impossible that Del had been gone eighteen years. He would have been nearly sixty years old. But the man she'd painted wasn't yet forty.

"What would he think of this world we find ourselves in today?"

Not much, she'd wager. Certainly he'd be saddened to learn that America was once again embroiled in war, and his heart would be broken by the civil unrest that reigned in the streets. But he would remind her that God reigned, even when it felt as if everything was careening out of control.

She trailed her fingertips along the top of the canvas, whispering, "And what would he think of his son?"

She smiled ruefully, knowing exactly how her husband would have answered that question. Del would remind her what *she'd* been like at Luke's age. Wild and headed for trouble. She'd run away from home, for pity's sake, when she was only fifteen. She'd been arrested and hauled back to River Bluff in disgrace. At least Luke hadn't done anything like that.

"God, please keep it that way. Bring him to You soon and save him unnecessary heartache."

She turned from the unfinished portrait, her gaze moving to the north wall of the studio, the only wall without windows. Here hung framed photographs that Luke had taken.

He had an innate talent with the camera, a talent that she'd encouraged him to develop. She'd allowed him to turn one of the downstairs rooms into a darkroom. But during the last year, the only photos he took revealed the disturbance in his spirit. His latest efforts were dark, ugly, depressing. Miriam hadn't included any of them on this wall.

She stared at one of her favorite black-and-white photographs. Luke had taken it the summer he was ten, only a month after receiving his first camera for his birthday. It was a family portrait of Miriam, her father and his wife, and Luke. Her son had directed them to sit in the living room on the sofa near the window. The morning light had filtered through the sheer drapes, creating a halo effect around the small group. They were all smiling, the image of the perfect American family.

Miriam shook her head. The perfect family, American or otherwise, was a myth. All families faced hardship or heartbreak of one kind or another.

Certainly that was true of her own. Her stepmother, Allison, had fallen the previous year and injured her knee. Surgery had failed to improve her condition, and she was now confined to a wheelchair. The strain of caring for his wife was beginning to show on Frank Gresham, now in his mid-seventies.

Miriam hated to admit it, but she had a few aches and pains of her own as she approached her fiftieth birthday. What she hated even more was that her vision had taken a nosedive this year, requiring reading glasses for any close-up work.

And then there was Luke. Troubled, rebellious, unhappy Luke.

"However does anyone make it through without You, Lord?"

Miriam returned to her chair, took another sip of coffee that had grown tepid, then settled in for a time of intimate communion with her Maker.

CHAPTER TWENTY-NINE

"Sanctuary!" Jacob cried, giving a fair imitation of Charles Laughton as Quasimodo.

Miriam laughed as she waved her friend inside.

"Go ahead. Mock me. You don't have to put up with all this wedding nonsense." He headed for the kitchen without waiting for an invitation.

"It isn't nonsense," Miriam said, following him.

He looked upward. "Why, God? Why did You bless *me*, of all men, with twin daughters?"

"Oh, Jacob, shame on you."

"Well, maybe. But did they *have* to fall in love at the same time, get engaged at the same time, get married at the same time? Tell me. Did they *have* to?"

"Sit down while I pour you some coffee."

"Thanks." He sank onto a chair. "Sorry about barging in so early on a Saturday morning, but I was in the way at home. A man underfoot is a pitiful sight."

"You're welcome anytime, Jacob. One more week, and this will all be behind you." Miriam handed him a mug filled with black coffee, steam rising from its rim. She had to admit that he did look frazzled. "Would you like some breakfast? I haven't eaten yet and was about to scramble some eggs."

"Luke not up?"

"He spent the night with a friend." She turned toward the stove, hiding her frown.

The past two weeks had gone rather smoothly in the Tucker home, all things considered, but last night she and Luke had had a horrible fight. She didn't like this new friend of his. Sean Lewis was his name. She couldn't put her finger on the reason for her distrust, but there was something about Sean . . .

"Hey, look at that!" Jacob said, breaking into her thoughts.

She turned to find him standing in the studio doorway.

"That's your finest portrait yet, Miriam."

"Thanks. I finished it yesterday."

"It looks just the way I remember Del." Jacob glanced in her direction. "Was it hard for you?"

She shook her head. "No. It was actually a pleasure. I recalled so many wonderful moments as I worked. Things he used to say and do." She shrugged. "I'd forgotten a lot of them, but they came back, one by one."

"What made you decide to paint it?"

"Luke."

Jacob raised an eyebrow.

Miriam walked toward him, stopping when the portrait came into view. "I wanted Luke to know the kind of man his father was. I was hoping, if I could show it in a painting, maybe—" She stopped herself abruptly.

Jacob placed his hand on her shoulder. "Do you want me to talk to him?"

"I don't know. I don't know what I should do. It seems like he keeps getting more and more angry and slips further and further away from me."

"Seventeen's a tough age for boys."

She nodded, then returned to the stove. "I give him to the Lord, and then I take him back, worrying and wondering what I should do. I'm trying to trust God with Luke's life, and yet I fear all the things that can go wrong."

"Parenthood."

"I suppose."

"You raised him right, Miriam."

"I wonder."

"Hey." He appeared at her side again. "If you've messed up in some way, God's able to rescue and restore."

Miriam gave him a wan smile. "Thank you, friend."

"My pleasure." He returned her smile. "That's what I'm here for. To be your friend, like you've always been mine." He put an arm around her shoulders and gave her a squeeze.

She felt herself tearing up. "Thank you, Jacob," she whispered hoarsely.

"Here. You sit down and drink coffee while *I* scramble the eggs."

Miriam was glad to oblige.

~

Later that morning, Jacob drove to his insurance office. His intention was to look up some information his CPA had requested, but he found himself ruminating about his life instead. He didn't know if his thoughts turned toward the past because Valerie and Victoria were getting married or if the portrait of Del was the impetus.

Jacob's eldest daughters had turned twenty-four this month. Funny, he'd once feared they would never get married. Now he feared their dual ceremonies would bankrupt him. Well, not really. God had blessed the McAllister family beyond anything a poor kid from River Bluff, Idaho, had any right to expect.

When he thought how close he'd come to throwing it all away . . .

He whispered a quick prayer of thanks. Not for the material things, pleasant though they were. No, his gratitude was for the love he and his wife shared and for the special bond he had with each of his children.

Jacob reached for the framed photograph on his desk. Luke had taken it last summer at the annual McAllister Insurance Company picnic in Ann Morrison Park. There they were, the McAllisters and the Tuckers, all the people he loved most in the world.

Jacob's gaze moved lovingly over each familiar face.

Elaine didn't look a day over thirty, although she was now in her mid-forties. True, she colored her hair to cover the gray, but her face was virtually unlined, and she was as trim as the day he married her, despite being the mother of five.

Valerie and Victoria had been blessed with their mother's good looks. Sweet and good-natured, they had strawberry blond hair, green-blue eyes, cute little button noses. Jacob had spent the better share of the sixties threatening to skin their boyfriends alive if they made any inappropriate moves on his daughters.

Mac, now eighteen, was the spitting image of his dad—tall and lean, outrageous carrot red hair, and those blasted eyebrows that had cursed more than one of his ancestors.

Poor kid.

But Mac was also one of the most genuine, caring people Jacob knew. An excellent student, the eldest McAllister son was in his first year of college, studying the law.

Ten-year-old Rachel and Bobby were in the fourth grade, and the true mischief makers in the clan. They had angelic faces, the better to deceive their innocent victims. God love 'em, they reminded Jacob more than a little of himself and Miriam when they were that age.

Speaking of Miriam . . .

Her image smiled at him from the photograph. Like Elaine, Miriam looked much younger than her true age. She'd filled out a little but hadn't gone to fat. What he liked best, however, was the joy that sparkled in her eyes of blue.

He remembered his boyhood love for her, how much he'd wanted her for his own. He'd been crazy with jealousy when she had married Del. But God had known what was best for both of them. He and Miriam were better as friends than they would have been as man and wife.

Lord, if there's something I can do to help Miriam with Luke, please show me what it is.

In the photograph, Luke stood on the fringe of the gathering, looking as if he didn't belong with the others. Everyone else was smiling broadly. But not Luke. He stared into the camera lens with a sullen expression that said, "I only set up this group photo because they made me. I want to be elsewhere."

Miriam had devoted her life to raising that kid and raising him right. She'd brought him up in the admonition of the Lord. From the cradle, Luke had seen by his mother's example that God should be the central focus of every day, every moment.

"Why Luke, God?" Jacob said aloud as he set the photograph on the desk. "My kids didn't have Christian parents when they were little or even a happy home life. Elaine and I were fighting all the time, and they took the brunt of it. But they've turned out well despite us, and they love You. Why is Luke turning such a hard heart toward You and his mom? And how can I help?"

If he was hoping for a flash of inspiration, it didn't come.

～

Miriam had given Luke strict instructions to be home by one o'clock in the afternoon. When he hadn't returned by five, she called the Lewis home. There wasn't any answer. She waited another hour, then tried again. Still no answer. She considered driving to Sean's, but then realized it wouldn't do any good if no one was home. All she could do was wait.

It was nearly ten o'clock before Luke straggled in the back door. Miriam was waiting for him, her arms folded across her chest, her emotions ping-ponging between relief that he was home and anger at his disobedience.

Before she could say a word, he looked up, saw her, and stopped. One look in his blurry eyes and she knew he wasn't sober.

"Lucas Delaney, what on earth have you been doing?"

"Nothing." He wobbled slightly before leaning a shoulder against the wall. "I was with my friends. Is that a crime?"

"You were supposed to be home hours ago."

"What for?"

"Because I told you to, young man." She narrowly held her temper. "You've been drinking, haven't you?"

He smiled, a twisted, mocking expression. "I'm stoned out of my gourd. So what?"

She covered her mouth with the flat of her fingers.

"You know what your problem is, Mom? You're uptight. You need to live a little." He pushed off the wall and walked unsteadily toward her. "Maybe you oughta try smokin' a joint yourself." He brushed past her. "I'm goin' to bed."

Miriam whirled around, no longer containing her anger. "You won't talk to me that way."

He muttered something about not talking to her at all and kept walking.

"Luke!"

He answered with an ugly curse before disappearing through the doorway.

Too stunned to move or speak, Miriam let him go.

~

Frank Gresham knew something was wrong.

Miriam hadn't been in church this morning, and she hadn't called him either. She *always* called him if she wouldn't be there.

He pulled to the curb, his automobile creaking and groaning as if it were as old as he was. Cutting off the engine, he stared at the front of Miriam's home while whispering a prayer. Then he opened the car door and got out.

Reaching the front door, he rang the bell and waited. After what seemed a long time with still no answer, he tried the door. It was unlocked.

"Miriam?" He poked his head inside. "Are you home?"

The house was unnaturally silent.

"Miriam?"

He moved toward the stairs, but a sound from the back of the house caused him to stop and listen. Yes, there it was again. Almost like a gasp for breath.

With a new sense of urgency, he headed for the kitchen. The back door was wide open. But before he got near enough to close it, he realized someone was in the studio.

"Miriam?" He stepped into the doorway.

The sight that met his eyes caused his old heart to miss a beat. Paint was splattered everywhere. On the drapes. On the walls. On the floor. And the canvases of Miriam's paintings had been slashed. Every single one of them.

Miriam knelt in the midst of the chaos, Del's ruined portrait held between her hands. She was wearing trousers and one of the baggy oversized shirts she liked to work in. Her feet were bare, her hair disheveled.

Frank awkwardly knelt beside his daughter, his old knees bending by sheer force of will. "What happened?"

She choked on a sob.

"Were you robbed? Are you hurt?"

She shook her head. "It was Luke."

"No!"

"Oh, Daddy." She hid her face against his chest. "What am I to do?"

She hadn't called him Daddy since she was ten years old. Frank held her close, patted her, stroked her, rocked her while she cried anew, deep, wrenching sobs, her tears wetting his shirtfront.

When at last the storm had passed, they got up from the floor, arms still around each other and made their way from the studio to the kitchen, where they sat at the table.

"Tell me what happened," Frank said gently.

"Luke came home drunk last night. I . . . I didn't say much to him then. He wouldn't have understood anyway. But this morning, I confronted him while he was still in bed. Maybe I should have waited for him to get up. I suppose I wanted to punish him in the midst of his hangover." She gripped Frank's hand and met his gaze. "He said horrible things, Dad. I didn't know he'd heard such words, let alone that he would say them to me." Tears welled again, threatening to spill over. "I demanded he get dressed and go to church with me. Then I went back to my room to try to calm down." She closed her eyes and dropped her chin toward her chest.

I'm too old for this, God. I think I've lived too long.

"It was like he went crazy," Miriam continued softly. "I heard things crashing to the floor and came running downstairs. Luke was ranting and cursing while he . . . while he slashed at the canvases with a knife and spilled supplies and knocked over tables and easels. I couldn't understand most of what he said, except that he hated me. He said he hated Del, too. He cursed the government and the war. I couldn't make sense of a lot of it, and I didn't try to stop him. I couldn't." A moan escaped her throat. "I was afraid of him, Dad. I was afraid of my own son."

Frank's chest hurt, like the weight of the whole world was pressing upon his heart. "Where's Luke now?"

"I don't know." She shook her head. "He ran out. I heard his car start. I guess he left."

"Miriam, I think we should call the police."

Her eyes widened. "I couldn't."

"He could be a danger to himself or someone else."

She seemed to crumple like a house of cards, her shoulders sagging. "Okay, Dad. If you think we should."

CHAPTER THIRTY

FOR THE FIRST TIME SINCE SHE'D MADE JESUS LORD OF HER LIFE, Miriam was angry at Him. She didn't pray. She didn't read the Bible. She still went to church, but it was a routine, not an act of worship. Inside, her heart had turned cold. Her ears were unable to hear, her eyes unable to see.

She didn't cry either. She hadn't shed a tear since the day Luke destroyed her studio and then left home, disappearing without a trace.

Many were the afflictions of the righteous. That was what God had told her years before. Well, losing her son was one too many afflictions. Whatever happened to the abundant life she'd been promised?

Nothing seemed to matter to Miriam now. Just getting out of bed was a chore. She hadn't put a paintbrush to canvas, refused even to enter her studio. Nor had she prepared her flower gardens for summer. Why bother?

She knew her father and stepmother were worried about her. Jacob and Elaine, too. Charlie and Rose Ireland, her pastor, friends at church, and even her neighbors were worried.

Miriam didn't care. Let them worry. She couldn't change how she felt. Her son was missing—he and his friend Sean—and her world had stopped turning on that dreadful morning seven weeks before.

~

The ringing of the doorbell startled Miriam. She'd been sitting in the living room, staring into space, while from the television set some reporter spewed more bad news.

"Police in Washington, D.C., arrested thousands of protesters who were blocking traffic in the nation's capital city in an attempt to stop government activities. After several weeks of antiwar demonstrations . . ."

The bell rang again.

Miriam didn't want to see anybody. She wasn't in the mood. Why couldn't everyone leave her alone?

Her visitor was persistent. The doorbell rang yet again, followed by knocking.

With a sigh, Miriam rose from her chair, turned off the sound on the television, then went to answer the door. If it was a salesman, so help her, she was going to give him a piece of her mind.

It wasn't a salesman.

It was Sean Lewis.

Miriam stared at the boy as if he were a ghost.

"Hello, Mrs. Tucker." He looked thinner. His long hair begged to be washed, as did the clothes he wore. Deep circles etched his eyes.

"Where's Luke?" She stepped onto the front porch and looked toward the street.

"He isn't here. He didn't come with me."

She met Sean's gaze a second time. "But he's all right?"

He shrugged.

Miriam grabbed hold of his arm, afraid he would leave before she learned what she needed to know. "Come inside."

He came without protest.

She took him into the living room and had him sit beside her on the sofa. "Tell me where he is."

"I don't know for sure."

"Then tell me what you do know." She fought to keep her voice level, but what she wanted to do was shake him until his teeth rattled. "Where have you been all this time?"

"San Francisco, mostly." His gaze dropped toward the floor. "We went down there to party, have a good time. We had some good trips, too." He shook his head slowly. "But then Luke got in with some guys that were doin' really heavy stuff and—" he stopped, looked at Miriam, shrugged again—"I got out. Decided to come back to Boise."

What he hadn't said frightened Miriam more than what he had said. She wasn't so out of touch with reality that she didn't understand that "good trips" and "heavy stuff" meant drugs. One look at Sean's face would have told her that.

"I . . . Luke was headed back east last I saw him. Him and some other guys."

"Back east?"

"New York, I think."

O God. Why so far?

Sean stood. "I better go. I gotta find me a place to crash for the night."

"You're not going home?" Miriam stood too.

"My dad threw me out. Said he never wanted to see me again, long as he lived." He shrugged. "I guess I knew I wouldn't be welcome. My old man's not the forgiving type."

Although Sean had tried to pretend otherwise, Miriam saw his hurt in his eyes. "Have you eaten, Sean? Are you hungry?"

He shook his head, but she suspected that was a lie.

She touched his arm again. "Come into the kitchen. I'll warm some leftovers."

～

Hours later, Miriam sat upright in bed, unable to sleep, her thoughts churning.

Heaven only knew why, but after feeding Sean, she'd felt compelled to offer him a place to stay for the night. She'd never liked the boy, had been convinced from the first that he was a bad influence on her son, and now he was staying under her own roof. For all she knew, he would rob her blind during the night.

What was I thinking?

As if in answer to her silent question, she looked at her nightstand. Or more precisely, she looked at the Bible on the nightstand. There was a thin film of dust on the burgundy leather cover, proclaiming the book's disuse.

If You could bring Sean back, why not bring Luke, too?

She reached for the Bible and placed it on her lap. With her right hand, she swept away the dust, then trailed her index finger over the small gold lettering in the lower right corner. *Miriam Tucker*, it said.

The Bible had been a birthday gift from Luke five years before. He'd earned the money to buy it by mowing neighborhood lawns and had been so tickled by her surprise.

She set the book on its spine and let it fall open at random. The book of Ezekiel. Her eyes were drawn to a highlighted passage: "I will feed My flock and I will lead them to rest," declares the Lord God. "I will seek the lost, bring back the scattered, bind up the broken, and strengthen the sick."

If that was meant to comfort her, it didn't. Her son was lost. He was scattered. He was broken and sick. She wanted him brought back now. She wanted him made whole.

Her thoughts warred with the words on the page, causing them to become muddled in her head. Reading was more an exercise of moving her eyes down one column, then the next and the next. But she kept going, as if she had no choice.

Ten or fifteen minutes passed, perhaps more, perhaps less. And then she read: "I will sprinkle clean water on you, and you will be clean; I will cleanse you from all your filthiness and from all your idols. Moreover, I will give you a new heart and put a new spirit within you; and I will remove the heart of stone from your flesh and give you a heart of flesh."

She blinked to clear her vision, only then realizing there were tears streaming down her cheeks.

I WILL REMOVE YOUR HEART OF STONE, BELOVED.

Remove my heart of stone. Forgive me. You are Lord, not I. Help me to see Your hand in this, but even if I can't, help me to remember You're in control.

She lifted her gaze toward her bedroom door.

I've blamed Sean for Luke's choices, and that was wrong of me. Take that root of bitterness and help me see Sean as You see him. A boy who needs to be loved. Not a troubled child. Just a child.

She sighed as she closed her eyes.

Behold, Your bondslave. Be it done to me according to Your will.

Julianna

Summer 2001

CHAPTER THIRTY-ONE

Jacob looked at Sean. "Lotta things've changed since then. Isn't that right, Senator?"

Senator? My eyes widened. *Senator Lewis? He was Miriam's Sean?*

I tried to envision this well-respected Republican senator as a drugged-out, runaway, troublemaking teen. I failed.

Jacob handed the campaign button back to Sean. "I always wondered. Did you vote for Nixon in '72?"

The senator chuckled. "I believe the privacy of the voting booth is still sacred, Mr. McAllister. You'll have to keep wondering." He looked at me. "It's because of Miriam that I didn't end up in a gutter somewhere. Or, more than likely, prison. She took me in, gave me a home after my dad washed his hands of me, saw that I finished my high school education, then helped me go to college." There was a sheen of heartfelt emotion in Sean's eyes. "She loved me and became a second mother to me. I owe her everything." He leaned forward and drew the box toward himself. "She showed me what was in here that first year I was with her. I learned a lot about the right way to live as she told me her stories."

I sensed I'd been learning, too, even if I wasn't sure exactly what.

"Some folks thought Miriam had more than her fair share of tough breaks. Maybe she did. But when life knocked her down, she looked up," Sean said.

"Looked up?" I said. "Don't you mean *got* up?"

Sean shook his head. "No, I mean *looked* up. She looked up to the Master and let Him put her back on her feet."

I shifted my gaze to the others. "All of you believe in God the same way Miriam did, don't you?"

"Yes," they answered in unison.

"And if I can be half as faithful as she was," Sean added, "I'll consider my life well lived."

I was afraid one of them would ask me what I believed about God and faith, and I didn't want to tell them I—

I what? What do *I believe?*

Rather than try to discover the answer to my own question, I changed the subject. "What's left in the box? I know there were some other things."

Sean gave me an enigmatic smile—looking every inch the successful politician—then reached in and withdrew the photo in a wrought-iron frame. His expression changed, became pensive, as he looked at it.

A flash of understanding hit me. "It's one of Luke's."

"Yes." He turned the frame toward me. "Of all the photographs Luke ever took, this one meant the most to Miriam."

"When did he come home? Was it very long after you?"

"Luke didn't ever come home."

I was horrified. "She *never* saw her son again?"

"Oh, she saw him, but it was many years later. And not here."

MIRIAM

AUTUMN 1988

CHAPTER THIRTY-TWO

MIRIAM LOVED THE MONTH OF SEPTEMBER. SUMMER WARMTH lingered in the daytime, but the crisp breath of autumn arrived with sunset. Flower gardens blazed in bright oranges and yellows, and tree leaves began to change colors overnight.

It was on one such late September day that Miriam Tucker sat in her backyard, reading a letter from her longtime friend, Sally Farnsdale, while young Chuck Ireland—Charlie's grandson—cut the grass.

Dearest Miriam,

How remiss I've been about staying in touch with you during the past year. It amazes me, the way every year flies by faster than the one before.

My daughter gave birth to our third grandchild, a little girl, two weeks ago, and I am writing this letter from their home in Pennsylvania. Samantha Joan has a full head of dark curly hair, but she is already beginning to lose it. I suspect it will grow back fair, the same as her mother and brothers.

My grandson Doug's Little League team was in the play-offs this year, and I was here to see it. I've enclosed a newspaper article that features a photograph of him after he hit a home run in the final game. (You'll have to excuse the bragging grandmother in me. I bought ten copies of that day's paper.)

Every time I see Doug play, I'm reminded of my brother. Douglas excelled at baseball, too. I can still remember how he fantasized about playing in the big leagues, but of course, World War II put an end to those dreams.

I don't know if you've heard that Tad's sister Nancy had a stroke last winter. She passed away in the spring. Tad was in River Bluff for the funeral, and his time there made him homesick for Idaho. Arizona was a nice interlude for us, but it isn't where we belong. Now that both the girls are living elsewhere with their families, there isn't much to keep us in Phoenix. Tad is planning to retire when he turns 55, and we want to travel and enjoy ourselves while we're still able.

The hardest thing will be leaving our wonderful church family in Phoenix. We've been blessed. The pastor, elders, and other leaders are so on fire for Christ, and Tad and I have grown enormously in our faith walk because of the teaching we've received. So God had His reasons for transferring Tad all those years ago, even if we couldn't understand at the time. But isn't that how it so often is?

Do write and let me know how you're doing. Your letters are always such an inspiration and encouragement to me. We'll be back in Phoenix by the time you receive this letter.
God bless,
Sally

Miriam set the letter on the patio table, then unfolded the newspaper clipping and studied the photograph. It was grainy, of course, but she could see the amazing resemblance of young Doug Stanton to his great-uncle.

Closing her eyes, she reflected upon her girlhood, recalling familiar faces, many of them—like her father—gone now.

"How fleeting life is, Lord," she whispered, looking once again at the clipping. After a moment or two more, she folded the paper in half.

On the backside of the article was an advertisement for a photography studio. Going Out of Business, it proclaimed. Everything Must Go. Beneath that heading were framed photographs—mountain ranges, sunsets, city streets, a Victorian-era house.

Miriam felt a tiny catch in her heart as she looked at the advertisement.

That's my house.

She held it closer and studied the picture. It looked so much like one Luke used to have hanging on his bedroom wall.

I must be getting senile. Why would a photograph of my house be in a Pennsylvania newspaper? I'm being ridiculous. Unless . . .

Her pulse began to race.

It wasn't possible. It was positively insane to contemplate the notion, even for an instant.

But contemplate it she did.

She walked into the house, clutching the clipping to her breast, went straight to the telephone, picked up the receiver, and dialed.

~

Sean Lewis pulled his Mercedes to the curb and cut the engine. Before opening the car door, he said a quick prayer for Miriam. He asked for wisdom for himself, too, so he would know the right things to say.

As a tax attorney, Sean spent his days dealing with facts. He liked to see things in black and white, liked to make things add up properly, liked to connect point A with point B in an orderly and direct manner. The likelihood of Miriam's finding Luke after more than seventeen years of silence because of a random newspaper clipping was too far-fetched to even consider.

But he would do just about anything for Miriam. He loved her that much.

He got out and strode toward the house, where he gave the

front door a quick rap. He wasn't surprised when it opened almost at once. He'd known she'd be waiting for him.

"Come in, Sean. Come in." Her blue eyes sparkled with excitement.

He obeyed, and she closed the door behind him. When she turned around, he placed his hands on her shoulders, leaned down, and gave her a kiss on the cheek.

"Did you call that investigator friend of yours?" she asked, not wasting a moment on pleasantries.

He nodded. "He's coming to my office in the morning. Why don't you show me that newspaper?"

"It's in the kitchen."

As Sean followed Miriam, he couldn't help thinking he hadn't seen so much spring in her step in a month of Sundays. He hoped she wasn't getting her hopes up too high, only to have them dashed.

As soon as he arrived at the kitchen table, Sean was handed the newspaper clipping. Miriam pointed to the photograph. "There. That's my house. I know it is."

"It does seem remarkably similar."

"Sean, it isn't similar. It's *this* house. Luke must be in Philadelphia. This could be his studio. We have to find him before the business closes and he disappears again."

Sean drew a deep breath, then met Miriam's gaze. "Even if it was taken by Luke, it's possible someone bought his photo and he has nothing to do with this particular business."

"It's possible." Miriam sat down. Her lips pursed, her expression thoughtful, her eyes staring into space, she combed the fingers of one hand through her short, white hair. Finally, she looked up again. "Years ago, God gave me a promise about Luke: 'Do not fear, for I am with you; I will bring your offspring from the east, and gather you from the west.' I didn't understand at the time, but I believe *now* is the fulfillment of that promise. God's bringing Luke home."

"I hope so, Miriam. You know I really do hope so."

CHAPTER THIRTY-THREE

MIRIAM HADN'T MAINTAINED LUKE'S ROOM AS A SHRINE TO HER SON as some mothers might have. In fact, the opposite was true. The bedroom had been used by many others in the past seventeen years. After Sean, other young people had made it their temporary home, some for short periods, some for longer. God had given Miriam a love and concern for youth in crisis, and she'd done what she could wherever and whenever God directed.

She supposed there were some who thought she'd been desperately trying to fill the vacancy left by her missing son, but she'd known that wasn't the case. God had healed her heart. She had missed Luke; she didn't deny that. But it was separate from her call to serve.

Oh, what joy she'd found in a life of obedience, in trusting God no matter the circumstances, in clinging tightly to the Savior. How she wished all Christians could discover the same joy. When God said He desired obedience rather than sacrifice, it was for their benefit. How often she'd ignored that truth while pursuing her own headstrong course.

Such were her thoughts as she stood in the middle of Luke's old room, one week after receiving Sally's letter. There were few traces of Luke in this room now—a few photographs on the wall, his bed and dresser, and the rolltop desk that had been Del's. Most of her son's remaining belongings—those things not given to charity—had been boxed and stored in the attic long ago.

Will I recognize the man he's become?

Sean was afraid she'd be disappointed, that the investigator would come up empty-handed, but Miriam *knew* the photograph belonged to Luke, and she *knew* she was going to see him again. She hadn't a shred of doubt.

Does he look even more like Del now that he's completely grown?

Luke would be thirty-five years old. He might be married, could be a father. He'd obviously continued with his photography. She wondered if he knew contentment in the life he'd chosen. She prayed that he'd been rescued from the bonds of drugs and alcohol.

She took pleasure in knowing he'd kept that photograph of the house. It meant he didn't hate her. At least she hoped that was what it meant.

She walked to the window and brushed aside the curtains to look down on the green sweep of lawn. In her mind, she heard the laughter of children at play, remembered the fun gatherings of friends this backyard had seen. Hard as it was to believe, most of those children in her memories had children of their own these days.

Am I a grandmother like Sally and my other friends?

Jacob and Elaine were grandparents to ten, all living within a twenty-five-mile radius. Bert Rey, Miriam's onetime beau, had three grandsons and a granddaughter. The Irelands had half a dozen grandchildren, and their first great-grandchild was expected around Christmas.

Wouldn't it be something if she had grandchildren to meet?

O God, help me be content no matter what we find. Keep Luke in Your tender care, wherever he is today. Let him know how much I love and miss him. Clear the way for our reconciliation, Jesus.

She let the curtains fall into place, then turned from the window, her gaze moving around the room.

I don't expect him to come back here to live. He's made his home elsewhere. He's not a boy any longer. But I would like to get to know him again. I'd like him to understand how much I love him, how much I've always loved him.

~

Three hours later, Miriam rode the elevator to the twelfth floor of the office building that housed the law firm of Price, Johnson & Lewis. Her old heart was racing.

"Wayne's here in my office," Sean had told her over the telephone a short while before. "We'd like to come to your house to talk to you. Say in about an hour?"

She'd known the waiting would drive her crazy. "If it's all right with you, I'll come there. It won't take me long."

The receptionist at the front desk greeted her with a smile. "Good afternoon, Ms. Tucker. How are you today?"

"Fine, thank you, Susan. And you?"

"Good, thanks."

"I believe Sean's expecting me."

"Yes, Mr. Lewis said for you to go right back." Susan pointed toward Sean's office.

"Thank you."

The door to the office opened before she reached it. One look at his face, and Miriam's heart plummeted. "What's wrong?" she asked as he reached out to take her hand.

He drew her inside and closed the door.

Following Sean's gaze, she turned toward the other man in the room, a fellow who looked to be in his forties—average height, brown hair that was thinning on top, a slight paunch.

"This is Wayne Scott," Sean said. "The investigator."

Wayne offered his hand. "Pleasure to meet you, Mrs. Tucker."

After shaking his hand, she looked at Sean. "What is it? What's he found?"

"Sit down, Miriam."

O God, please . . .

With a hand on Miriam's shoulder, Sean gently urged her into a chair; then he pulled a second chair close to hers rather than going around and taking the one behind his desk. It seemed an ominous sign.

Don't let Luke be dead. Please, Father.

"Miriam—"

"Is he dead?"

Sean shook his head. "No."

"But?"

He exchanged a look with Wayne.

"Tell me the truth, Sean. All of it. I don't want it sugar-coated."

It was Wayne Scott who answered, "Mrs. Tucker, the photography studio in Philadelphia isn't owned by your son. It belongs to his . . . partner."

"If they're business partners—"

"Not his business partner," Sean said, taking one of her hands between both of his.

She looked at him, confused.

"His . . . companion." Sean cleared his throat. "Miriam, Luke is living in a homosexual relationship."

"That can't be." She shook her head. "It's not true. He had girlfriends. He went out on dates. Luke wasn't gay. I would have known. A mother would know such a thing."

Wayne flipped open a steno pad and glanced at his notes. "When your son first arrived in Philadelphia, he was heavily involved in the drug scene. That was in the mid-seventies. He was using everything." He paused but didn't look up. When he continued, his voice was softer, as if he didn't want Miriam to hear. "He was picked up for male prostitution a couple of times."

"No," Miriam whispered.

Now the investigator met her gaze. "It's how a lot of addicts earn money to pay for their drugs, ma'am. When you're strung out, you'll do anything. It's a sad fact of life on the street." He glanced at his notes. "Your son was in drug and alcohol rehab in the spring of 1980 and, from all accounts, has stayed clean and sober ever since." Wayne flipped the notebook closed.

A heavy silence squeezed the air from the room.

"What's his name?" Miriam asked at last.

"Whose name?"

"Luke's . . . friend."

"Teague," the investigator replied. "Keegan Teague. He's from Pennsylvania. Same age as your son."

Her chest felt as if it were being crushed beneath some horrid weight.

"How long have they been together, Mr. Scott?"

Silently, she marveled at what a normal thing that was to ask in the middle of this nightmare.

Wayne Scott checked his notes again. "Since '83."

How am I supposed to react, God? It goes against everything I believe in. What do I say to Mr. Scott and to Sean? This is my son we're talking about. This is Luke.

"Mrs. Tucker," Wayne continued, "in the past eight years, since he got clean, Luke's done well for himself with his photography. He's made a lot of money. But what impressed me during my investigation was the way people talked about him as a person, about his many kindnesses, the way he's reached out to others and helped in his community."

Miriam remembered her little boy, the child who had worked beside her in the garden, the one who had run errands for their elderly neighbors.

Wayne leaned toward her, speaking softly. "One lady called him a real-life hero. Others used words like *gentle, integrity, compassionate, humble, intelligent, fun.* He cares about others a lot more than he cares about himself."

Yes, that was the boy she remembered. Not the troubled teen who'd run away from home. If only . . .

"It didn't seem everybody knew about Luke's . . . lifestyle choice. He kept that pretty quiet." Wayne glanced toward Sean. "Up until this year."

Sean squeezed Miriam's hand.

She knew. Somehow she knew what he was going to say even before he said it. She wanted to stop him. She wanted to stop everything. She wanted to place her hand over his mouth and force him to swallow the hateful words.

"He's dying, Miriam. He's got AIDS."

Someone screamed, *"No!"* She supposed it was her own voice, although it sounded otherworldly and far, far away.

~

Miriam flung herself at the foot of the Cross. She grabbed for the hem of Christ's robe and held on for all she was worth. Jesus was her anchor in this storm-tossed sea, her only hope as she faced a situation that seemed completely hopeless.

CONSIDER IT ALL JOY, MY BRETHREN, WHEN YOU ENCOUNTER VARIOUS TRIALS, KNOWING THAT THE TESTING OF YOUR FAITH PRODUCES ENDURANCE. AND LET ENDURANCE HAVE ITS PERFECT RESULT, THAT YOU MAY BE PERFECT AND COMPLETE, LACKING IN NOTHING.

Joy? I don't feel joy. I feel helpless and lost and crushed. I'm afraid of what's coming. Help my faith produce endurance and have the perfect result. O God. O God. How can I lack nothing when I know my child is dying?

IF YOU LACK WISDOM, BELOVED, ASK ME. I GIVE GENEROUSLY AND WITHOUT REPROACH.

I need Your wisdom, Lord. I have none of my own. I'm drained. I'm empty. I don't know what to think or to feel. I don't understand.

BLESSED ARE YOU, MIRIAM, MY BELOVED, WHEN YOU PERSE-VERE UNDER TRIAL; FOR ONCE YOU HAVE BEEN APPROVED, YOU WILL RECEIVE THE CROWN OF LIFE, WHICH I, YOUR LORD, HAVE PROMISED TO YOU WHO LOVE ME.

I do love You, Lord. I do love You.

Miriam held on. She held to the Cross until it seemed she could feel slivers of wood embedded in her palms. Nothing would make her let go.

Not even the loss of her only child.

JUST BEFORE FIVE O'CLOCK ON A STORMY OCTOBER AFTERNOON, Delta Airlines flight #1930 descended through thick, black clouds and landed on the rain-washed runway. From her seat in the first-class cabin, Miriam said a silent prayer of thanksgiving for their safe arrival in Philadelphia.

Not that her arrival would be a welcomed event.

Miriam had been told by Luke's companion, Keegan Teague, not to come. She'd been told Luke didn't want to see her.

She came anyway.

I WILL BRING YOUR OFFSPRING FROM THE EAST, AND GATHER YOU FROM THE WEST.

I've been gathered from the west, Lord. Here I am.

She glanced to her left. Dear Sean. He'd insisted on joining her, wouldn't take no for an answer. She'd tried to convince him that she would be fine on her own, but she was glad he hadn't believed her. She needed his moral support, just as she needed the prayers of her loving church family in Boise.

Sean offered comfort with a smile.

The plane came to rest at its gate. The seat-belt sign went dark, the Jetway rolled into place, and the exit door opened. Minutes later, Miriam and Sean walked into the airport terminal.

An unexpected tremor of dread passed through her, followed by an overwhelming sense of weariness. She must have staggered slightly, for Sean reached to support her with his arm.

"Miriam, we're waiting until morning to find Luke's house."

"But—"

"This isn't up for discussion," he interrupted sternly. "We'll get our luggage, pick up our rental car, and go straight to the hotel. You can get room service to bring your dinner and then get a good night's sleep."

She nodded, knowing he was right, knowing she couldn't face more than that just yet. As prepared as she'd thought she was to see her son again, she suddenly knew she wasn't prepared at all.

She was weak and vulnerable and afraid.

~

Miriam stared out the rental car window as Sean drove through the Philadelphia suburb. Behind tall trees, now shedding leaves of gold, stately homes proclaimed the affluence of those who lived within.

"Are you sure we're on the right street?" she asked.

"I'm sure."

After a few moments of silence, Miriam said, "Mr. Scott said Luke's done well, but I didn't expect this."

"It's pretty impressive."

"What if he won't see me?"

"Don't give in to fear, Miriam. Let's trust God to work out the details."

She sighed. "My soul clings to Thee," she whispered, quoting a verse from Psalms that she'd read that morning.

She envisioned herself, as she had ever since that fateful day in Sean's office, lying prostrate at the foot of the cross, her hands clasped tightly around its base.

BE STRONG IN ME, BELOVED, AND IN THE STRENGTH OF MY MIGHT. YOU ARE WEARING MY ARMOR, THAT YOU MAY STAND FIRM AGAINST THE SCHEMES OF THE DEVIL.

She felt like the Israelites preparing to cross the Jordan. They must have worn armor. They must have prepared in many ways for battle. They'd faced something unknown. They'd been told to follow the ark of the covenant, keeping it in view, so they would know the way by which they should go, for they had not passed that way before.

Neither have I passed this way before, Lord. Show me the way. You're the ark of the new covenant, Jesus. Help me follow You into this unknown land.

The car slowed.

"That's it," Sean said. "That cream-colored brick on the right."

Miriam stared at the two-story house with the ivy-climbing trellises on both ends. The lawn was faultlessly manicured, the landscaping a true work of art. There were two cars parked in the circular driveway—a black Lincoln Town Car and a silver Rolls-Royce.

All the trappings of success. All the *things* that money could buy. But none of it could save her son from the disease that ate away at his body.

O God . . .

Sean turned into the driveway and followed it to the front door. After cutting the engine, he looked at her. "Ready?"

She shook her head.

He gave her an encouraging, albeit sad, smile, then said, "Sure you are. Because you're not alone."

This time she nodded, then reached for the door handle.

Sean prayed silently as he walked beside Miriam toward the entrance of the home. He was nervous, afraid both for Miriam and for Luke.

He'd felt more moments of guilt these past few weeks than he cared to count. After all, he'd played a role in Luke's addiction to drugs. They'd smoked pot together and dropped acid together. Sean hadn't participated in Luke's destruction of Miriam's art studio, but he'd egged him on. And while Luke had continued his downward spiral in the ensuing years, separating himself from the mother who loved him, Sean had been taken into her home and into her heart. Though the hardness of their hearts had kept Sean's parents from forgiving or forgetting before their deaths in a 1979 traffic accident, Miriam had forgiven him completely. Sean had been loved and cherished, taught new values, and shown a better way.

Would any of that have happened if Luke had returned to Boise, too? Not likely. God was sovereign, of course, and could have found another person to give Sean the love and guidance he'd needed. But the truth remained: He'd been the beneficiary of Luke's absence for all these years.

And he felt guilty for it.

~

The doorbell was answered by a muscular, broad-shouldered black man.

"Mr. Teague?" Sean inquired.

"No. May I help you?"

Sean's hand alighted on Miriam's shoulder. "We're looking for Luke Tucker. This is his mother."

The man's eyes widened in surprise as his gaze shot back to Miriam. "His mother? I didn't think Luke had any family."

"He does," Sean answered.

"I'm Rick Joyner, Luke's nurse." He held the door open wide. "Come on in."

Miriam let out a breath she hadn't known she was holding, relieved she wouldn't be turned away.

"Come in," Rick said again. "I'm glad you're here. Luke doesn't have many guests these days."

Miriam stepped into the entry hall. "Luke isn't expecting us." She swallowed hard. "He may refuse to see me."

Rick's gaze was filled with understanding and kindness.

Softly, she added, "I haven't seen or heard from him in over seventeen years."

"Then maybe we'd better not tell him you're here. We'll just go right up."

Miriam glanced toward Sean, who nodded.

"He's having one of his better days," Rick said as he motioned for Miriam and Sean to follow him. "But his appearance will probably shock you. That's why he's cut himself off from his friends. Luke hates being treated like an invalid, even though that's exactly what he is." He glanced over his shoulder. "Try to act as normal as possible."

Miriam understood what he was doing. He was preparing her for the worst. She could have told him that nothing prepared a mother to see her dying child.

She was thankful for Sean's gentle support, his hand cupped beneath her elbow, as they climbed the stairs to the second story.

DRAW NEAR TO ME, MY DAUGHTER, AND I WILL DRAW NEAR TO YOU. LOOK INTO MY FACE. FIX YOUR EYES UPON ME.

Yes, Lord.

BELOVED, I FORMED LUKE'S INWARD PARTS. I WOVE HIM IN YOUR WOMB. HE IS FEARFULLY AND WONDERFULLY MADE. HOW PRECIOUS ARE MY THOUGHTS TOWARD HIM. WILL YOU TRUST ME?

Yes, Father, I'll trust You.

Rick stopped before reaching a half-open door. He looked over his shoulder, questioning her with his eyes.

"Though I walk in the midst of trouble, Thou wilt revive me;

Thou wilt stretch forth Thy hand against the wrath of my enemies, and Thy right hand will save me. The Lord will accomplish what concerns me; Thy lovingkindness, O Lord, is everlasting; Do not forsake the works of Thy hands."

Peace welled up inside. Peace, yet it came with a power that left her awed. She knew she'd felt the touch of God.

"I'm ready."

He gave a nod, then pushed open the door. "You have visitors, Luke." He walked toward the bed. "They've come a long way to see you."

Miriam drew a deep breath, then followed the nurse into the bedroom.

The man in the hospital bed was gaunt, dark half-moons etched beneath his eyes. His head had been shaved. Or perhaps his hair had fallen out. Miriam heard a wheezing sound with every breath he took. His frail body barely disturbed the blankets that covered him. He looked old. So very, very old. She realized then that she'd expected to see her boy, her Luke, the teenager he'd been before he ran away.

A part of her mind was screaming. A part of her heart was shattered. But God sustained her.

Rick raised the head of the bed, then placed an extra pillow behind Luke. "It's time we had some company, isn't it? My jokes were getting stale."

Her son squinted at her, and she wondered if his vision was bad.

"It's me, Luke," she said, trying to keep her voice from quavering. "It's Mom." She moved to the opposite side of the bed from Rick. "I've missed you, darling." She wondered if he would allow her to take hold of his hand.

"You shouldn't have come." He closed his eyes, as if those few words had drained the last of his strength. "I don't want you to see me like this."

She took his hand, unable to keep from it, and leaned forward. "I'm not leaving, Luke. I love you. I want to be with you. I want to help you."

"It's too late to help me," he whispered.

"No." She fought the tears. Later she would cry. Later when she was all alone in the safety of her hotel room, she would cry to God, pouring out her pain. But not now. She didn't want to cry now. "It isn't too late, Luke. There's still time for you to be loved. There's still time for you to know the Author of love."

The despair in his eyes when he met her gaze stole her breath away.

"Let me stay, Luke. Please let me stay."

CHAPTER THIRTY-FIVE

KEEGAN TEAGUE MET MIRIAM AND SEAN UPON THEIR RETURN THE following morning. "Why'd you come now, Mrs. Tucker?" he asked before the front door closed.

Miriam didn't find the question strange. After all, Keegan had lived with her son for five years. He must know Luke hadn't seen or talked to her since he left home so long ago. Keegan had reason to be suspicious.

"Look," Sean said, a hint of anger in his voice, "we aren't here to—"

She stopped Sean's retort with a touch on his arm. "I came because I love my son, Mr. Teague."

He eyed her warily.

"Has he said he wants me to leave?" Miriam asked.

Keegan shook his head. "No."

"Then I'd like to be with him in the time that remains." She glanced toward the stairway. "I want him to know how much I love him. That's all."

"We won't get in your way, Mr. Teague, or cause you any trouble." Sean placed a protective arm around Miriam's shoulders and drew her close to his side.

"I believe you." Keegan turned, walked to a side table, where he picked up a shoe box, then returned to Miriam and Sean. He held the box toward Miriam. "I think you should read these. They're addressed to you. Maybe they'll help."

She took the box but didn't look inside.

"I'll be out the rest of the day." Keegan grabbed his briefcase that was sitting on the floor. "Rick knows how to get ahold of me if I'm needed." He opened the door. "You don't have to stay at the hotel. There's room for you here, if you want." Then he left.

Miriam was surprised by his abrupt departure.

"He won't be around much," said a voice from behind her.

She turned to see Rick Joyner standing on the stairs, midway between the upper and lower floors.

"Keegan's scared and angry about what's happening," he continued. "He's having a hard time handling all of this, so he stays away as much as he can. He uses work as an excuse."

"I thought he was closing his studio," Sean said.

Rick descended the rest of the way. "He is. Plans to leave Philadelphia, I understand. Just as soon as he can."

Just as soon as Luke's gone, Miriam amended silently.

"I came down for some coffee. Would you like some?"

Miriam shook her head. "No thanks. I'll go up, if it's all right."

"Sure. Luke's sleeping, but you can sit with him if you like."

Sean stayed behind, and Miriam was grateful. She wanted to be alone with her son. She needed time to pray for him, time to gather her thoughts.

Luke's bedroom was as large as the living room in Miriam's Boise home. The ceilings were extra high, making more space for the many framed photographs that hung on the walls, most of them nature shots. Photographs, both large and small, some black and white and some in color. There was one of a lake at sunset, another of a stormy sea, another of majestic mountain peaks capped with snow.

He sees Your magnificent creation, Lord. Now let him see You, the Creator.

Miriam walked slowly to Luke's bedside and sat in the nearby chair, her gaze fastened to his face. She tried to ignore the various machines that were placed around the bed, machines that beeped and whirred as they monitored the ebbing life of her son.

Lord Jesus, he knows about You because I told him when he was a boy. Now I want him to know *You. To really know You. I long for him to take You into his heart and into his life. God, Your word says Jesus hasn't lost one that the Father gave Him, so I'm trusting You not to lose Luke.*

She prayed for several more minutes, then sat in silence, simply watching her son, remembering him as the boy he'd been. At long last, she glanced at the shoe box on her lap and lifted the lid with trepidation.

The box was filled with envelopes, many of them sealed and stamped. All of them were addressed to her. She opened one and began to read.

~

June 1981
Dear Mother,

How many times have I tried to write this letter, and how many times have I ripped it to shreds? I keep searching for the right words, and they never seem to be there.

Your son is a homosexual. There it is, in black and white.

It frightens me, writing this to you. I don't know how you feel about me after all these years. I don't know if you've forgiven me for running away like I did, let alone if you can forgive me for this.

Can you? I'm not sure I can forgive myself . . .

~

After she'd read the first, she opened the next letter.

June 17, 1983
Dear Mom,

Today is my 30th birthday, and I've been thinking about you. Can't get you off my mind. Three different times I picked up the phone to call you, and three times I hung it up again.

You were always so sure of who you were. You always said it was who you were in Christ that mattered.

Well, I've never been sure of anything. I've been loaded down with guilt and self-loathing for so many years . . .

~

December 25, 1984
Merry Christmas, Mom,

It's cold and snowy in Philadelphia, and I'm remembering when I was a kid and was in Cub Scouts and Bert Rey was the cubmaster. The pack went snowshoeing in McCall over Christmas break, and I came home half frozen. You made a fire in the fireplace, and we sat on the floor—you and me—and toasted marshmallows on coat hangers while I thawed out. Remember?

Keegan and I are spending a quiet Christmas at home. That's the way it usually is, mostly because we both still have "two sets" of friends, those who know about us and those who don't. Fear of rejection drives us into seclusion . . .

~

May 1988

I'm dying, Mom. I've known for a long time. I've wanted to tell you. All these unmailed letters. I've got a box full of them, telling you what's happened to me over the years, telling you that I'm gay, telling you that I've been successful with my photography and thanking you for buying me my first camera. None of that matters now. Maybe the letters don't matter now either. Maybe you'll read them after I'm dead and buried. Maybe you'll never know. Maybe life isn't supposed to make sense. Maybe this is all there is . . .

~

Miriam wiped the tears from her eyes, then refolded the last of the letters and returned it to the shoe box. She felt tired, too tired even to move the box from her lap to the floor.

O God, help me.

She looked toward the bed and discovered Luke watching her. Her heart skittered and her stomach knotted.

"You look old." He sounded surprised.

She smiled tenderly. "I *am* old."

"I didn't think you'd change." He closed his eyes. "I always saw you staying the same."

He hasn't much time left. Her heart was filled with a sense of urgency. *God, help me know what to say.*

"You read the letters." His breathing was labored, and it was obvious how much effort it took to speak. "You must hate what I am. I know what you believe."

Miriam took hold of his hand. "I'm here because I love you, Luke. Not to condemn you. I'm here to remind you that God loves you, too."

Luke tried to pull free of her grasp, but she didn't let him.

"If God loves me," he whispered hoarsely, "why'd He make me this way?"

Miriam felt a moment of panic. How could she answer? She didn't know what to say. The gay rights protesters she'd read about in the papers and magazines said they were born that way. Were they? And if they were, then how could God judge them?

Like an electrical current, the Lord spoke the answer into Miriam's heart, and she, in turn, spoke to her son.

"God didn't create *any* human being to sin, Luke. What He made was good and right and perfect. We're each one of us fearfully and wonderfully made. God created us to fellowship with Him. He loves us and longs to be with us."

Luke tried again to pull free from her grasp, and again he was too weak to succeed.

"Luke, we're sinners, all of us, because we live in a fallen world. The human race was given free will, and we chose to sin. All of us choose it, each in his own way. But your sins, whatever they are, are no greater than mine. And God made a provision for us, a way of escape, a way for us to break free of whatever bondage Satan would trap us in." She leaned closer, speaking softly but forcefully. "Luke, you know the way to freedom. You've known it in your heart since you were a young boy."

He turned his head on the pillow so she couldn't see his face. "It's too late for me. This is what I am, and this is the way I'll die."

"But it isn't too late. All you have to do—"

"It's too late!" With what little energy he possessed, Luke jerked free of her hold. "Leave me be."

CHAPTER THIRTY-SIX

TIME AND AGAIN, DESPAIR DESCENDED UPON MIRIAM, AND
time and again, she refused to give it a foothold. She stayed in
Luke's room, sitting at his bedside, praying quietly, reading
aloud to him from her Bible, occasionally singing songs of praise
to God. She didn't know if her son heard or not, but she prayed
his spirit did.

She was vaguely aware of the comings and goings of Rick
as he tended to Luke. She was barely aware of Sean sitting on a
small sofa on the opposite side of the room, most likely praying
for her as well as for Luke.

Time held no meaning for her as she waged spiritual warfare
on behalf of her son.

～

The hour was late, the bedroom cloaked in the shadows of night
except for the small reading lamp beside Miriam's chair and the
glowing green, red, and yellow lights on the monitors.

"'He who dwells in the shelter of the Most High will abide
in the shadow of the Almighty,'" she read. "'I will say to the
Lord, "My refuge and my fortress, My God, in whom I trust!"
For it is He who delivers you from the snare of the trapper, and
from the deadly pestilence. He will cover you with His pinions,
and under His wings you may seek refuge; His faithfulness is a
shield and bulwark.'"

Thank You, Lord.

"'You will not be afraid of the terror by night, or of the arrow that flies by day; of the pestilence that stalks in darkness, or of the destruction that lays waste at noon. A thousand may fall at your side, and ten thousand at your right hand; but it shall not approach you. You will only look on with your eyes, and see the recompense of the wicked. For you have made the Lord, my refuge, even the Most High, your dwelling place. No evil will befall you, nor will any plague come near your tent.'"

Lord, drive out this plague from my tent. You are a covenant God, and I pray in the power of Your righteousness, not my own.

"'For He will give His angels charge concerning you, to guard you in all your ways. They will bear you up in their hands, lest you strike your foot against a stone. You will tread upon the lion and cobra, the young lion and the serpent you will trample down.'"

Reveal Yourself to Luke. Bear him up.

"'Because he has loved Me, therefore I will deliver him; I will set him securely on high, because he has known My name. He will call upon Me, and I will answer him; I will be with him in trouble; I will rescue him, and honor him. With a long life I will satisfy him, and let him behold My salvation.'"

Finishing the psalm, Miriam closed her eyes and pressed her Bible against her breast. She heard the soft ticking of the mantel clock above the fireplace. She heard the hated beeps and whirring of the machines. She heard the raspy breathing of her son.

What more can I do, Jesus? What more?

"Mrs. Tucker?"

She opened her eyes to find Rick standing beside her chair, leaning close.

"Why don't you let me read to him for a while?"

"No, I want—"

"You're exhausted. Let me help."

"Well, I—"

"Maybe we should let him know what heaven's going to be like."

She hesitated.

"The twenty-first and twenty-second chapters of the book of Revelation make it pretty clear."

"You're a believer?"

He nodded.

"Thank You, Jesus," she whispered as she reached out to touch the side of Rick's face. "You are an answer to a mother's prayers."

"And you're an answer to mine."

Curious, she asked, "How long have you been caring for my son?"

"I arrived three weeks ago."

"Three weeks." A wave of awe washed over her. It had been three weeks since she'd received Sally's letter.

DO NOT FEAR, FOR I AM WITH YOU; I WILL BRING YOUR OFFSPRING FROM THE EAST, AND GATHER YOU FROM THE WEST.

In a whisper, she said, "You've been praying for Luke the whole time, haven't you?"

"Yes, ma'am."

She held her Bible toward Rick. "Read to him about heaven. I want him to know."

~

They continued like that for five days and nights—Miriam and Sean and Rick—taking turns reading the Bible aloud, taking turns praying. Most of the time, Luke seemed unaware, but occasionally, he appeared to listen.

It was midmorning of the sixth day. Miriam sat alone in Luke's bedroom while Sean slept in another room. Rick had left the house to run a few errands. Keegan still spent most of his time at the studio, avoiding the sickroom.

In a voice made gravelly from too many hours of use, Miriam read from Second Corinthians. "But whenever a man turns to the Lord, the veil is taken away. Now the Lord is the Spirit; and where the Spirit of the Lord is, there is liberty. But we all, with unveiled face beholding as in a mirror the glory of the Lord, are being transformed into the same image from glory to glory, just as from the Lord, the Spirit."

"What liberty?"

She swallowed a gasp as she looked toward the bed. The appearance of death was written on Luke's face.

"What . . . liberty?" he asked again, speaking with difficulty.

Miriam rose from her chair, stepped to the bedside, and clasped his frail hand in both of hers. "You shall know the truth, and the truth shall make you free. Jesus is the truth, Luke. All you have to do is reach out to Him."

"You don't . . . know . . . what I've . . . done."

She leaned forward, staring hard into his eyes, speaking urgently. "My darling boy, it doesn't matter what you've done as long as you ask Jesus to cleanse it all away."

"Too . . . late."

"No. No, it isn't." She tightened her grip on his hand.

Unblinking, Luke stared at her, and in the depths of his eyes, Miriam saw the desire to believe, the need to hope.

"Remember the thief on the cross, Luke. It was the eleventh hour. He was dying. He couldn't do anything to make up for his sins. He couldn't change a single moment of the life he'd lived or the choices he'd made. It was too late for him, too." She drew his hand to her lips and kissed his knuckles. "Only it wasn't *really* too late. He called upon Jesus to remember him in His kingdom, and Jesus did."

Her son shook his head, almost imperceptibly.

"Luke, listen to me. Time is growing short. Don't hold yourself apart from God a moment longer. Satan has already stolen your life here on earth. Don't let him have your eternity." Her voice rose, tinged with anger. "Don't let him steal that from you, too."

Luke's eyes widened a fraction.

Tears welled, and her vision blurred. A lump formed in her throat.

"I . . . give up," he whispered.

Miriam blinked, wanting to see him clearly, *needing* to see him clearly.

His eyes drifted closed, and he rolled his head to the side, away from her.

O God, not yet. Not yet.

For a long time, neither of them spoke, neither of them moved. Miriam would have thought he was gone, except the machines continued to make the same sounds as always.

Finally, she heard a sweeter sound. The sweetest sound of all. In a voice too soft to be called a whisper, Luke spoke the name: "Jesus." Then he slipped from consciousness.

CHAPTER THIRTY-SEVEN

For the next forty-eight hours, Luke didn't stir. The doctor advised Miriam that it was doubtful he would awaken again.

As if he'd sensed Luke's time was near, Keegan didn't leave the house that morning. It was just before noon when he entered Luke's bedroom and softly said, "May I speak with you, Mrs. Tucker?"

"Of course."

He motioned with his head toward the opposite end of the room, then led the way. Once Miriam arrived, he turned to face her, his expression grim. "Look, I know what you think about me and Luke. About the way we live."

"I don't believe you do."

"Yeah, right. I've heard the intolerance of your type before."

Miriam drew a deep breath before speaking. When she began, her voice revealed her sorrow. "Mr. Teague, it's true that I disapprove of the lifestyle you and my son have lived. I disapprove because God's Word says it's a sin."

He flushed with anger and opened his mouth to speak.

Miriam lifted a hand to stop him. "Hear me out. Your relationship with my son is no worse in God's eyes than a man and a woman having sex outside of marriage or a father teaching his child it's okay to keep the extra nickel a clerk mistakenly gave in change. Sin is sin. Lust is as evil as adultery. Anger toward a brother is as evil as murder. God doesn't rank one sin as lesser or greater than another. He hates them all."

Her reply seemed to catch Keegan unaware, surprise him, confuse him.

"Sin separates mankind from a holy God, but while God hates sin, He loves the sinner. He loves us so much He sent His Son to die for us." She reached out and touched his forearm. "That's the only real truth there is."

"Miriam," Sean said from Luke's bedside. "I think he's waking."

She hurried across the room, followed by Keegan. She took the hand Sean offered her and leaned into him for support, involuntarily holding her breath as she stared at her son.

Luke's eyelids fluttered. A soft groan sounded in his throat. Miriam glanced at Rick, who stood at the foot of the bed, but he was also watching Luke.

She bent forward. "Luke, honey, we're here with you. We're all here. All of us who love you. It's okay. Whatever happens next, it's okay. Jesus is with you. He loves you most of all."

Luke opened his eyes then, meeting her gaze. She could tell it was a struggle for him to focus. He rolled his head to the side, looking toward the opposite side of the room. "Pho-to," he rasped.

Miriam followed his gaze to the dresser. It was covered with photographs, as was the wall above it. She took his hand. "Which one, Luke?"

"There." He tried to lift his free hand, but it fell limply back upon the mattress.

Sean left her side, walked to the dresser, and while looking over his shoulder at Luke, slowly touched first one, then another, then another, each time asking, "This one?"

Finally, Luke whispered, "Yes."

Sean brought the photograph, encased in a wrought-iron frame, to the bed.

"Give . . . Mom."

Miriam took it from Sean.

"Look . . . at . . . it."

She did as he'd asked. It was a black-and-white shot of a spectacularly rugged mountain range. It had been taken at sunset or sunrise, and the sunlight reflected off a body of water, forming a brilliant cross of light between camera and background.

"Home," Luke wheezed.

"Yes, it reminds me of Idaho, too." She returned her gaze to Luke. "Are these the Sawtooth Mountains? Or maybe the Tetons?"

"No. Home." Somehow he found the strength to lift his hand, and with his index finger, he touched the photograph right in the heart of the cross. "Home."

Miriam began to weep. She hadn't meant to. She'd wanted to wait a little longer, but it wasn't to be.

Her thoughts tumbled back through time. She remembered standing by another hospital bed, remembered another man who'd told her he was going home. She'd argued with Del. She'd begged him not to leave her. She'd wanted her own way. She'd wanted to keep him with her, no matter what.

She wouldn't do the same with his son. She would trust in God instead.

"I understand, Luke," Miriam said as she leaned close to him, smiling through her tears. "You can go home now. It is well."

Julianna

Summer 2001

I KNEW BETTER THAN TO SAY ALOUD WHAT I WAS THINKING: THAT it wasn't fair. Miriam Tucker, poor woman, had lost all the people she'd loved most—her brother, her husband, her parents, and finally her son. All but her father had been tragically young when they died. It seemed more heartache than any one person should have to suffer in a lifetime.

I pondered the things Miriam had told her son as he lay dying, and I found I wanted to believe that her words were true. That it wasn't too late. Not too late for me. Not too late for my life.

Christy spoke, interrupting my musings. "It's gonna feel weird, another family living in this house. Dad remembers coming here to play as a kid when Grandpa and Mrs. Tucker were dating. He told me about the barbecues and the croquet games they used to have with a bunch of the neighbors and different folks from church."

A lightbulb went on in my head. This girl was Andy Rey's daughter, Bert's granddaughter. I had to wonder why she was included in this group. She was so much younger than the others.

As if to answer my silent question, Christy lifted the last item—the serving tray—from the box. "I learned so much from Mrs. Tucker in the months I was with her." She brushed her hand lightly over the tray. "This is the only thing in the life box that she didn't pick out herself. I put it in there after she died. It just seemed . . . right." She shrugged. "You know. Like when we remember her life, we ought to remember it all."

MIRIAM

JULY 3, 2001

CHAPTER THIRTY-NINE

MIRIAM AWAKENED EARLY, BEFORE SUNRISE WAS MORE THAN A promise in the eastern sky. Her bedroom window was wide open, and she heard the meadowlark announcing the dawn from the trees in her backyard.

Good morning, Lord. I see You've brought me through another night. I thank You for Your provision.

She sat up in bed, slowly lowering her legs over the side. Then she rose and shuffled to her favorite chair near the window. Her bones protested each and every step.

It isn't that I mind getting older, Lord, but the process is no picnic.

She took her favorite Bible from the table beside her. The leather cover was cracked with age and some of the pages were coming loose. She let the book fall open in her lap. The page corners were bent, the edges soiled from constant thumbing and flipping. Some passages were highlighted and underscored, and there were notes written in the margins, some dated, some not.

Your Word sustains me, O God.

She put on her glasses but didn't begin reading just yet. Instead, she turned her gaze out the window to watch as the sky changed the wispy clouds from pewter to peach to startling white.

The last dawn of my seventies. How can that be?

Friends were planning a surprise eightieth birthday party for her tomorrow. Supposedly they were coming for a Fourth of July barbecue, but she'd guessed what they were up to. She might not have the sharp vision she had when younger, but she could still read their faces well enough. Not to mention those hushed conversations whenever two or more came for a visit.

You've been good to me, Your handmaiden. You gave me a family when I had none of my own. You've blessed me with so many to love, so many to love me. I'm thankful for them all.

One advantage of growing old was that a person had time to reflect. For Miriam, that reflection brought many reasons to praise God.

Her bedroom door eased open, drawing her gaze toward it just as Christy poked her head in.

"You're up early." Christy pushed the door the rest of the way open. She was still in the oversized T-shirt and plaid boxer shorts she slept in. Her short hair stuck out in every direction, and her eyes looked bleary.

"I'm always up early. But I'm surprised *you* are."

Christy yawned and ruffled her hair with one hand. "I've got a ton of things to do. Thought I'd better get to it."

"You young people always take on too much. So many plans, always in a hurry."

"And you weren't in a hurry when you were my age?"

"Well . . ." Miriam chuckled softly. "Come to think of it, maybe I was."

Christy turned toward the door. "Want anything special for breakfast?"

"No, dear. Whatever you fix will be fine."

"Then it'll be French toast and bacon." The girl left the room, still looking half asleep.

It was good to have someone else living in the house again, although Miriam hadn't been happy with the reason. A bad fall a year ago had damaged her hip, and instead of getting better, it had steadily worsened until Miriam had a difficult time seeing to her daily needs.

Ever faithful, the Lord had brought Christy to her door at just the right time. Otherwise, she feared she would have had to move into one of those retirement villages. She shuddered at the thought. She wasn't ready to give up her home. She was comfortable here. So many memories. Over half of her lifetime had been spent within these walls.

Christy had come to Boise to attend the university, and her father had insisted she pay a call on Miriam. After Bert died some years back, Andy and his family had moved to Oregon, and Miriam had lost touch with them. Then suddenly there was little Christy, standing on her front porch, like an answer to prayer. Miriam needed someone to live with her, and when she offered a room to Christy, the girl was quick to leave the dorm and move in with Miriam.

She's the granddaughter I never had, isn't she, Lord? Thank You for sending her to me.

Miriam closed her eyes and leaned her head against the back of the chair.

You're a God of the smallest details and design, and I'm in awe. Way back in the beginning of my life, You knew the end because You were already here. How intricately You planned it. How carefully You've provided what I needed when I needed it. You withheld those things that would have harmed me, and You brought into being those things that were for my good.

She smiled, remembering Christy's question: *"And you weren't in a hurry when you were my age?"* Oh my, yes. She'd been a reckless, strong-willed girl, and there was no denying it.

Funny, wasn't that only yesterday?

～

The front page of the morning paper had a color photograph of United States Senator Sean Lewis on his return from a diplomatic trip overseas. There he stood, waving at the camera, his wife one step behind him.

Miriam studied the photo with a sense of pleasure.

In his late forties, Sean wore the mantle of leadership well. "Compassionate conservatism" was how one reporter had described Sean's ideology.

Not that he didn't have his detractors. Sean was a man who stood by his principles and beliefs. He didn't compromise in matters of ethics or integrity, and he cast his votes in accordance with his Christian worldview. That could—and oftentimes did— make him unpopular in some segments of Capitol Hill. But the voters in his district admired him, and he'd won his second term to the senate by an overwhelming majority.

But it was the night of his first election that held one of Miriam's fondest memories.

"There isn't anybody in this room," Sean had said from the podium in the Riverside's ballroom, "who doesn't know that I was a kid looking for trouble, and I found plenty of it. Since the newspapers dug up that part of my history before even *I* knew I was running for office, you've read all the gruesome details. But I'd be remiss if I didn't publicly thank the person responsible for turning my life around before I messed it up completely."

He'd held out his arm toward Miriam, who was seated nearby, watching him with tear-blurred eyes.

"Miriam Tucker," he'd said, talking to her instead of to all his campaign supporters who were jammed into the ballroom, "you loved me when nobody else would, because I wasn't very lovable, and you showed me the more excellent way. You did it by example, not just by words. I watched you live it, day in and day out. No matter what came your way, I saw you rejoice in God. Thanks, Miriam, for being a mother to me when I needed a mother, for being a friend when I needed a friend, but most of all for being a witness for God's truth when I needed God."

My goodness, she was crying as she recalled his words. She

dabbed her eyes with a tissue, then put her glasses in place and read the newspaper article.

If I live long enough, she thought when she was done, *I just might get to address him as Mr. President.*

Now wouldn't that be something.

CHAPTER FORTY

THE TELEPHONE RANG AT A QUARTER AFTER TEN THAT MORNING.
Miriam answered it on the eighth ring. "Hello?"

"Oh, thank goodness you're all right."

Miriam moved her walker off to the side and sank onto the
chair next to the telephone. "How are you, Sally?"

"That was my question."

"I'm perfectly fine. I just wasn't near the phone."

"You need a cordless to carry with you. What if you were to
fall and couldn't call for help?"

"Sally Farnsdale, you're a worrywart."

The other woman laughed. "I suppose I am."

"Christy takes good care of me. I'm fortunate to have her
here."

"She's the fortunate one, Miriam. I was thinking only yesterday what an impact you had on my life."

"Me?"

"Of course, you. Don't you remember when I was going out
with Hadley?"

Miriam shook her head slowly. "Hadley Abernathy. I'd
forgotten that young man."

"Tad and I, we raised our girls to know there are natural and
spiritual consequences for the things they say and do, for the
choices they make." She cleared her throat. "Do you realize
that's one of the most important lessons I learned as a teen?
And you taught it to me, Miriam."

The words warmed her heart. "How kind of you to say so."

"Not kind. Just true." There was a moment or two of silence before Sally continued, "Listen, I was wondering if it would be all right for me to come a bit early for the barbecue tomorrow. I'd like to do my baking there rather than haul it from River Bluff."

"Of course it's all right, Sally. I always enjoy your company."

"Great. I'll be there around noon."

"Good-bye, Sally. I'm looking forward to tomorrow."

~

The mailman came at eleven-thirty, delivering a package, three bills, and at least a dozen colorful card-sized envelopes.

"Your birthday, Mrs. Tucker?" He set the package on the entry-hall table, then handed her the rest of the mail.

"Tomorrow, Mr. Jones."

"Don't worry. Turning thirty isn't so bad."

"I'm glad to know that, young man," she replied with a laugh.

He gave her a wink. "Well, you have a great one, and if there's any cake left over, you know where to find me."

"I'll save you a piece."

Whistling softly, Mr. Jones turned and strode down the sidewalk.

After closing the front door, Miriam dropped the mail into the pouch on her walker, then pushed the walker into the living room. Sunlight filtered through leafy trees outside the windows, making the room bright and cheerful.

Thanks for the sunshine, Lord.

It was fun going through the cards. There was one from the women's Bible study she had attended up until the last year; it was signed by all ten members of the group. There was one from

Rose Ireland, who had retired to Florida after Charlie died. There was one from Andy Rey and his wife, and one from each of Jacob McAllister's five children and their families.

The ninth card she opened was from Philadelphia, but she didn't need the return address to recognize Rick Joyner's handwriting. They'd been exchanging letters regularly for more than a decade. Although, come to think of it, it had been nearly a year since she'd received a letter from him.

She smiled as she read the humorous birthday greeting inside the card, then unfolded the accompanying slips of white stationery.

Dear Mrs. Tucker,

Sorry it's been so long since I last wrote to you, but when you hear the reason, you'll rejoice with me.

I've begun the most incredible new adventure. At 45, God's called me out of the nursing profession and into full-time ministry. He's plunked me down in a storefront church in Philadelphia. It's the last place I expected to be, I'll tell you that. God has a way of changing our human plans to meet His divine one, doesn't He?

I spent a lot of time serving Him, when what He wanted was for me to spend time loving Him. I used to think the eternal life He offered was a destination, a place I'd get to in the future. But then He showed me, through something you said a couple years ago, that eternal life isn't a place or a destination. It's a relationship, a fellowship. "This is the way to have eternal life—to know you, the only true God, and Jesus Christ, the one you sent to earth" (John 17:3).

Who knows how many times I've read that without really seeing what it said. But I do now, and it changed the course of my life.

So here I am, called out of my comfort zone and into the work He prepared for me. I don't know what's waiting in my future, but that's okay. As long as I stay in touch with Jesus, I don't need to lean on my human understanding. Makes for a pretty exciting time.

One last thing before I close. While leading an evangelism class at the church, I met a terrific woman whom God has shown me is to be my wife. I haven't actually proposed to Sharon yet, but I think she knows, too. If I were a gambling man, I'd lay odds you've been praying for this to happen. Am I right?

Have a great birthday on the 4th. (Hope this letter reaches you before instead of after the festivities.) Write soon. I promise to be better at my correspondence.
Love in Christ,
Rick

Miriam smiled as she refolded the letter, then closed her eyes.

O Father, how awesome this is. How exciting, all that You're doing in Rick's life. Thank You for sending him a helpmeet. I didn't know You'd called him into full-time ministry, and now I see You've directed my prayers for a wife for him because he'll need someone to work at his side.

Miriam never ceased to be amazed by how much God cared for His children, how much He longed to pour out His blessings upon them.

Her thoughts drifted again, meandering through the years, so many twists and turns made clear in hindsight. She saw the many times God had worked things for good when the enemy had meant them for destruction. She envisioned the faces of friends and loved ones. She recalled how often God had used someone to touch her heart, to encourage her, to build her up and set her back on the right path again.

"Even when I am faithless," she whispered, "You, O Lord, are faithful to me."

CHAPTER FORTY-ONE

JACOB MCALLISTER CAME BY WITH LUNCH AS HE DID EVERY Monday, carrying bags of takeout from his favorite deli. Usually Elaine came with him, but today he was alone.

"Her arthritis is acting up again," he said when Miriam inquired about his wife. "I told her to rest since she'll see you tomorrow at the barbecue. No point putting herself out today."

"Same could be said for you."

"And miss eating German sausage and fried potatoes with onions?" He set the large white sack on the kitchen counter. "Not on your life."

Miriam shook her head. "Elaine will have your hide if she finds out. All that fat." She clucked her tongue.

"Well then, don't tell her." He took two plates from the cupboard. "She worries too much as it is."

"Jacob McAllister, you know you're supposed to watch your cholesterol."

He sighed dramatically. "Remember the good old days when nobody gave a thought to cholesterol levels?"

"Remember the good old days when it wasn't uncommon for folks to die in their sixties instead of living as long as we have?"

Jacob glanced over his shoulder. "Okay, you got me there." Then he shrugged and proceeded to dish up their lunch.

"Stubborn old goat."

"You betcha."

After a companionable silence, Miriam asked, "Did you see Sean's picture in the morning paper?"

"I sure did. You must be poppin' buttons."

She chuckled in agreement.

Jacob carried the plates to the table, then sat opposite her. Their gazes met momentarily before they bowed their heads and he blessed the food.

Following their "Amens," Miriam picked up her fork. "Did you imagine we'd still be friends when we were this old?"

"I never figured we'd get *old*, let alone *this* old."

"I guess you're right about that."

In her mind, she saw the two of them as if it were only yesterday, standing by the river, she longing to leave for Hollywood and begging him to go with her, Jacob insisting he had to stay behind.

"You know, my friend," she said softly, "my life's been a bigger adventure than I ever dreamed it would be."

"Even without Hollywood?"

So, he'd been remembering, too. "Even without Hollywood." She moved the food around the plate with her fork. "God has been good to me."

"Only one thing you ever lacked, far as I can tell."

She looked at him. "What's that?"

When he raised his hands in an exaggerated shrug, she saw again the redheaded kid from sixty-five years before. "You never had the extreme pleasure of being Mrs. Jacob McAllister," he answered with a wink.

"Oh, you. We'd have driven each other crazy before two weeks were out."

"True."

～

After Jacob left, Miriam took a nap in the easy chair in her studio.

She dreamed of the River Bluff of her youth. She dreamed of her parents and Arledge, of Chief Jagger and Pastor Desmond, of Jacob, and of Del and Luke. Even in her sleep, she knew it didn't make sense that Luke was there with his dad and the others, but it pleased her all the same, seeing them together.

Suddenly she was no longer in town but standing by the river. Although she couldn't see herself, she knew she was young again and wearing a swimming suit. She could feel the sun beating down upon her shoulders. The water, though swift, looked inviting.

"Come on in!" she heard someone shout, but when she looked around, she was alone.

Her heart hammered as she stepped closer to the river's edge.

"Come on in, Miriam!"

She wanted to. She was ready to. She drew a deep breath and . . .

The slamming of the back screen door jerked her awake. Moments later, Christy appeared in the kitchen, several plastic grocery bags in hand.

"Hey, Mrs. Tucker. Sorry it took me so long. Have you had lunch?"

Miriam placed a hand over her racing heart. "Yes, dear. Jacob was by as usual."

Christy said something else, but Miriam wasn't listening. She was thinking about the river in her dream and wishing she'd had time to dive in.

~

Sean called on the telephone just before suppertime. For several minutes, he answered Miriam's questions about his diplomatic trip, describing the different terrains and cities and customs. Finally, he said, "Want to know the most important thing I learned while I was away?"

"Of course I do."

"Freedom is worth whatever it costs, and it *always* costs somebody something."

She thought of Arledge, who'd died young in the name of freedom.

"But there was more the Lord wanted to show me during this trip," Sean continued. "He wanted me to understand that only when I'm bound to Him am I really free. I thought a lot about how the men who guided our nation in the beginning put the Creator into our founding documents, but today we can't mention Him. Those men wanted us to have freedom *of* religion, and instead it's become freedom *from* religion. Especially from Christianity. How'd we get to this state?"

"Pride. I believe pride's at the root of all mankind's ills."

He agreed with her, then abruptly changed the subject. "Are you ready for the Lewis clan to descend upon you tomorrow?"

"My goodness, Sean. There's nothing I like more than seeing you, Pam, and your three little ones. I miss the children so much when you're all in Washington."

"They miss you, too. Well, better run. Pam's calling me to supper."

"Tell her she looked lovely in the newspaper photo."

Sean laughed. "I'll tell her. See you tomorrow, Miriam."

"Tomorrow, dear. Good night."

"Good night."

CHAPTER FORTY-TWO

SHORTLY AFTER CHRISTY CAME TO STAY WITH MIRIAM, THEY'D established a nightly routine of herbal tea and quiet conversation before retiring. This night was no different.

Christy set the small tray—one she had decorated with stickers and Bible verses—on the table near the window, then removed the cozy from the pot and poured tea into the two delicate china cups. After handing one to Miriam, who was seated in a wing-backed chair, Christy sat on the matching footstool. She balanced her saucer on one knee while blowing across the surface of her cup before taking a sip.

Miriam wondered what lay before this young woman in the years to come. Unlike Miriam—who at the same age had been all wrapped up in the things of the world—Christy Rey was grounded in the Lord. That anchor would serve her well. Still, Miriam prayed that God would keep her from any unnecessary valleys and from the wiles of the evil one.

Finding Miriam watching her, Christy grinned and asked, "Excited about your birthday tomorrow? I mean, not everybody lives to be eighty years old."

"I suppose I'm surprised, more than anything."

"Surprised? Why's that?"

"In here—" she tapped her temple—"I'm only about thirty-five." She glanced at her wrinkled, liver-spotted hand, the one holding the china cup. "Outside, of course, I look every one of my eighty years."

"Have you minded getting older?"

Miriam pondered the question a short while. "Not the way you mean," she replied at last. "The aches and pains, the unsteady hands, the failing eyesight—those aren't fun. But there's something . . . reassuring . . . about this season of life, too. Maybe it's knowing the time is growing near to be in heaven with the Lord."

"Don't say that! You're going to live lots longer. Years and years and years."

"Oh, my dear girl. I'll live just as long as the good Lord wants me to, and not one instant more."

Christy frowned.

Miriam set her cup and saucer on the tray, then leaned back in her chair and gazed out the window as dusk painted her backyard in shades of gray. "I was reading in Ezekiel before you came in, about the river flowing from the temple of God."

She sensed more than saw Christy reaching for one of several Bibles on the nightstand.

"Chapter forty-seven," Miriam said, still staring out the window. "Verse one."

Christy opened the Bible and began reading: "'Then the man brought me back to the entrance of the Temple. There I saw a stream flowing eastward from beneath the Temple threshold. This stream then passed to the right of the altar on its south side. The man brought me outside the wall through the north gateway and led me around to the eastern entrance. There I could see the stream flowing out through the south side of the east gateway. Measuring as he went, he led me along the stream for 1,750 feet and told me to go across. At that point the water was up to my ankles. He measured off another 1,750 feet and told me to go across again. This time the water was up to my knees. After another 1,750 feet, it was up to my waist. Then he measured another 1,750 feet, and the river was too deep to cross without swimming.'"

"Stop there. Do you see what He's saying?"

"Well . . ." Christy studied the passage of Scripture, concentration furrowing her forehead as she worried her lower lip between her teeth.

Miriam closed her eyes, remembering her dream from that afternoon, a dream of a different river, the river of her youth. *"Come on in!"* Her pulse quickened at the memory.

"Don't ever stand on the edge, Christy. We're led to the river of life because God wants us to swim in it." She opened her eyes again and met Christy's gaze. "My dear, dive into the life God has for you. Never be satisfied with splashing around near the bank, where the water's only up to your ankles. Swim!"

Christy slipped from the footstool onto her knees beside Miriam's chair. She took hold of Miriam's hands, squeezing gently. "I will, Mrs. Tucker. I promise."

~

It was after midnight, and Miriam lay awake in her bed.

Eighty years, Lord. How quickly they've passed.

As clear as if it were only yesterday, she remembered the time her father had taken her by the hand as they'd walked along the sidewalk in River Bluff. *"You've only just begun your life, Miriam. I want you to live it well."*

Live it well.

Did I, Jesus? Did I live it well?

AND THE ANGEL SHOWED ME A PURE RIVER WITH THE WATER OF LIFE, CLEAR AS CRYSTAL, FLOWING FROM THE THRONE OF GOD AND OF THE LAMB . . .

Her old heart fluttered with excitement. She could see the

crystal-clear river in her mind, just as she could feel God's Word reverberating in her heart.

AND THEY WILL SEE HIS FACE . . .

Jesus, my Lord.

She ventured forth. Step by step by step, she moved into the rushing river, out into the deep water. It felt deliciously cool and wonderfully familiar.

Familiar, as if she'd been swimming there for a long, long time.

Then she realized she wasn't alone. Someone was with her, Someone holding her up, as He had throughout the years.

YOU LIVED IT WELL, MIRIAM, MY BELOVED DAUGHTER. WELL DONE, MY GOOD AND FAITHFUL SERVANT. WELCOME HOME.

JULIANNA

Autumn 2001

"CONGRATULATIONS." OUR REAL ESTATE AGENT, MARCY Arnold, dropped the keys into Leland's open hand. "Enjoy your new home."

"We will," he answered, smiling at me, love in his eyes.

We waited until Marcy left the front porch; then Leland unlocked the door and motioned me to enter.

As I stepped onto the parquet floor of the entry hall, my mind was flooded with memories of the first time I'd entered Miriam Tucker's house. I'd had no idea how hearing about her life would alter mine for eternity. I'd had no notion that before I left on that fateful day, I would know Jesus as my Savior and Lord.

But that's exactly what had happened.

I took a deep breath. A hint of rose petals. A little musty. A dash of old age and disuse. Just like the first time.

Suddenly I remembered something else about that day. I'd wanted a chance to begin again, to get a clean slate. I'd wanted a "do over."

And I got one, didn't I, Lord? I got my "do over." It's a new life in You.

I took a step toward the living room. "Thanks, Miriam," I whispered, a smile on my lips and joy in my heart. "See you when I get there."

ABOUT THE AUTHOR

Author Robin Lee Hatcher, winner of the Christy Award for Excellence in Christian Fiction and the RITA Award for Best Inspirational Romance, has written over thirty-five contemporary and historical novels and novellas. There are more than 5 million copies of her novels in print, and she's been published in fourteen countries. Her first hardcover release, *The Forgiving Hour*, was optioned for film in 1999. Robin is a past president/CEO of Romance Writers of America, a professional writers organization with over eight thousand members worldwide. In recognition of her efforts on behalf of literacy, Laubach Literacy International named The Robin Award in her honor.

Robin and her husband, Jerry, live near Boise, Idaho, where they are active in their church and Robin leads a women's Bible study. Thanks to two grown daughters, Robin is now a grandmother of three ("an extremely young grandmother," she hastens to add). She enjoys travel, the theater, golf, and relaxing in the beautiful Idaho mountains. She and Jerry share their home with Delilah the Persian cat, Tiko the Shetland sheepdog, and Misty the Border collie.

Readers may write to her at P.O. Box 4722, Boise, ID 83711-4722 or visit her Web site: www.robinleehatcher.com.

TURN THE PAGE FOR AN EXCITING PREVIEW
OF ROBIN LEE HATCHER'S NEXT BOOK

FIRSTBORN

AVAILABLE FROM

TYNDALE HOUSE PUBLISHERS

SUMMER 2002

August

The late afternoon sun glared down upon the floating dock, baking the wooden plank surface and the three sunscreen-slathered teenagers who lay upon it, their feet dangling in the water. For the moment, the three of them were alone in the small inlet, the speedboat having taken another run up the length of the reservoir, pulling skiers in its wake.

Opening her eyes, Erika James glanced at the brown hills that surrounded Lucky Peak Reservoir, noting how little time was left before the sun slipped beyond them. Maybe a couple of hours at most.

She wasn't ready for the day to end.

She wasn't ready for the summer to end.

But she couldn't stop either of those things from happening any more than she could stop her boyfriend, Steven Welby, from leaving Boise tomorrow, headed off for his first year at the University of Oregon in Eugene.

Her sixteen-year-old heart was breaking. No, it had already broken. She felt as if she could curl up and die.

She rolled her head to the right to look at Steven. His dark brown hair, still damp from his last turn behind the boat, was plastered against his scalp. He'd worked for a lawn maintenance company all summer, and his skin had turned a dark golden brown.

As if sensing her gaze upon him, he smiled but didn't open his eyes. Her heart tumbled and her pulse raced.

Erika had fallen in love with Steven Welby the moment she first laid eyes on him. That had been last September, the third week into her sophomore year at Borah High School. She'd been heading from her second-period algebra class to her third-period biology class, and he'd been walking toward her.

Anna Smith had nudged Erika and said, "Wow! Look at him. Wouldn't I just die to have him ask me out?"

Steven Welby. Senior class president. Track star. All-around athlete. Probably the most popular student in the school.

Steven hadn't asked Anna Smith out, but he had asked Erika. And she'd about died for the pure joy of it, just as Anna had said. Neither Erika nor Steven had dated anyone else for the past ten months. Considering the short leash Erika's dad kept her on—11:00 P.M. curfew with no exceptions, not even for school dances; no unchaperoned parties; no out-of-town excursions—Erika thought it amazing that Steven had stuck around for a month, let alone ten of them.

"You guys thirsty?"

Erika rolled her head to the left.

Dallas sat up, squinting despite his dark-colored Ray-Ban sunglasses. "I'm gonna swim over and see what's left in the cooler. Want me to bring you something?"

"Nothing for me," Steven mumbled, sounding as if he'd been asleep.

Erika shook her head. "I'm okay, too."

Dallas Hurst was Steven's best friend, had been since they were in first grade, and the two of them were almost always together. Because of it, Erika spent nearly as much time with Dallas as she did with Steven. There were probably some people who didn't know for sure which of them was her boyfriend.

But Erika never would have fallen for Dallas. Not that he

wasn't charming or good-looking. In fact, he was *too* charming and *too* good-looking. He always had girls hanging around him, flirting with him, hoping to become his girlfriend, but none succeeded. Erika didn't think he'd dated the same girl more than two or three times since she'd known him. Dallas was a player. He didn't waste himself on girls who wanted anything more than a good time.

Dallas stood, stretched, then dove into the water and swam toward shore.

Erika turned her head back toward Steven. His eyes were open now, and he was watching her. She felt that wonderful-terrible fluttering sensation in her stomach.

Oh, yes. She loved him. Loved him more than life itself. And she was scared because he was going away. He was going away without promising he would return to her, without asking her to wait for him. He would spend his days with pretty, sexy college girls, girls who were willing to do more than just kiss.

Had she made a horrible mistake, refusing him when he'd wanted more from her?

"Come here," he commanded gently.

She rolled onto her right side and into his waiting embrace. He pulled her close, kissing her, slow and sweet, and she wished for another day, another week, another month before he went away. Maybe if she had more time, she could make him say he loved her, make him ask her to wait, make him propose.

Steven drew his head back slightly, ending the kiss. "Oregon isn't so far away. I'll come home for holidays, and we'll see each other then."

"Thanksgiving is three months away."

"It'll go fast."

"No, it won't," she whispered, afraid she might start crying. "I'm going to be so lonely."

He kissed the tip of her nose. "Dallas'll still be here. Maybe the two of you can get together occasionally."

"Maybe," she answered.

But Erika didn't believe that would happen. Dallas would have his hands full with the coeds at Boise State. He wasn't going to have time to spend with his friend's old girlfriend, a mere junior in high school.

Besides, it wasn't Dallas she wanted to be with. It was Steven and only Steven. But he was going away in the morning, leaving her behind with her broken heart.

Erika was certain she would never be happy again.

CHAPTER ONE

June, twenty-three years later

"Oh, Steven! Ethan would love it." Erika Welby stared at the automobile—a 1955 red-and-white Chevy sedan with pristine whitewall tires. "It looks just like the one you had in high school. But can we afford it?" She glanced at her husband.

Steven jerked his head in the direction of the garage door. "Ask them. They're the buyers."

Erika whirled about to find Dallas and Paula Hurst standing near the open doorway, both of them grinning like Cheshire cats.

"Don't refuse, Erika," Paula pleaded. "We want to do this."

"You know we love the kid." Dallas draped his right arm around Paula's shoulders. "It'll be a great surprise for his seventeenth birthday."

It would, indeed. Ethan had wanted a car of his own ever since obtaining his driver's license. And this one—an exact replica of the car his dad had owned at the same age—would be his dream car. But with college expenses looming on the horizon and a single-income budget—

"Aren't you the one who's always saying it's more blessed to give than to receive?" Dallas lifted an eyebrow, challenging Erika. "Are you going to rob us of this blessing?"

Erika knew Dallas and Paula could easily afford to buy the car. They didn't have any children, and both of them were highly successful professionals—Dallas in the computer field and Paula in real estate development. Dallas was Ethan's godfather and had always doted on the boy. Would it be so wrong to accept his generous offer?

She looked at Steven again. His hopeful expression reminded her so much of their son that she simply had to grin. That seemed to be answer enough for him.

He turned toward their friends. "Okay."

Dallas and Steven let out identical whoops and stepped toward each other for a high-five slap. Then they headed off to strike a deal with the salesman.

Paula's laughter drew Erika's gaze. "Do you suppose the two of them will ever change?"

"Never," Erika replied, shaking her head.

Steven and Dallas had been best friends since grade school. They'd played baseball together, tormented their sisters together, learned to golf together, been sent to the principal's office together—just to name a few things. After Erika had become Steven's girlfriend, they'd gone on more dates with Dallas as a third wheel than they had with just the two of them. Erika hadn't minded; Dallas had become her pal, too. When Steven and Erika got married, Dallas had served as best man. Steven had returned the favor years later. The two friends had never lived more than five miles apart, with the exception of the time Steven was away at college.

But those weren't years Erika liked to remember, even now.

Paula rescued her from unpleasant memories by asking, "Is this as much like Steven's old car as the guys say it is?"

"Yes." Erika turned toward the automobile. "It's identical. Could be the same one, for all I know." She ran her fingertips along the driver-side door. "Steven kept his car shining clean, just like this. He was so proud of it. He worked awfully hard to earn the money to buy it."

A frown puckered Erika's forehead. Would the car mean more to Ethan if he had to work for it the same way his dad had?

"Oh no!" Paula exclaimed. "Look at the time. I've got an appointment in twenty minutes. I'll never make it if the streetlights aren't with me. Tell Dallas I had to run." She raised her hand in a half wave. "See you Saturday." Then she hurried away, her high heels clicking against the concrete floor.

Erika stared after the younger woman, feeling suddenly dowdy.

Paula Hurst—thirty years old, petite, slender, and as pretty as any cover model with her short red hair, cat green eyes, and pouty lips—lived a high-paced life, a wireless phone in one hand and an electronic organizer in the other. Since the first day Dallas brought Paula to meet his friends, Erika had never seen her looking anything but totally put together—makeup on, hair perfectly coiffed, nails manicured.

"I haven't been totally put together since Ethan was born," Erika muttered as she turned toward the Chevy again.

Seventeen years. How was it possible that Ethan was about to have his seventeenth birthday? Where had the time gone? It seemed only yesterday since she'd cradled that squalling, red-faced newborn in her arms; only a moment ago since she'd sat in the rocking chair at 2:00 A.M. and watched him nurse; a second in time since she'd worried about fevers, coughs, and spit-up, healthy baby checkups and keeping current with immunizations. When did her baby boy get to be big enough to ride a bike, let alone drive a car?

"I'm going to be blubbering in another minute." She closed her eyes. *Thank You, Lord, for the gift of my son. Watch over him as he becomes the man You designed him to be.* She released a deep breath, her brief prayer making her feel better. And not a moment too soon.

Steven jingled the car keys as he reentered the garage.

"Sweetheart, it's ours. Wanna drive into the foothills and smooch awhile? No bucket seats in this lady."

"Oh, sure. That would set a good example for Ethan, wouldn't it?" Her refusal couldn't dim the pleasure she felt at her husband's suggestion. Truth was, after eighteen years of marriage, Steven still made Erika go weak in the knees. "Besides, you've got to get back to work."

"It's a mighty nice day for a drive," he cajoled. "I could play hooky."

"Is this car for Ethan—" she playfully punched him in the arm— "or are you trying to relive your wild and wooly youth, Mr. Welby?"

He grabbed her and pulled her close. "Both," he answered. And then he kissed her.

~

Steven whistled an old Righteous Brothers tune as he opened the front door to Parker Elementary and entered the building. All was quiet now that school had let out for the summer.

Jessica Shue, the school secretary, lifted her gaze from the papers on her desk. Seeing who it was, she picked up two message forms and held them out to him. "These are for you."

"Thanks." He took them, glanced at the names on each slip, then continued toward the door with his name stenciled on the milk-white glass: *Principal Welby*. He couldn't help it. He grinned. There was something about those two words that made him feel good.

He supposed there were those who would consider him something less than successful, if not an out-and-out failure. At forty-one, he didn't make a huge salary. He didn't have a large savings account. He didn't own a big house or a fancy boat or an expensive car. What he had was a wife he adored and a son he was proud of, a cozy house with a low mortgage, two cars that they owned free and clear, and a job he enjoyed going to every day.

Now how many men his age could say that?

He sat in the chair behind his desk, glancing at the messages again. The first was from his pastor regarding the men's meeting in two weeks. The other was a reminder of his semiannual dental appointment. Neither call needed to be returned.

He swivelled the chair toward the window, looking out at the empty schoolyard. Sprinklers shot arcs of water across the grass. Muddy puddles pooled beneath the monkey bars. Several robins hopped about, searching for worms.

He missed the kids. There was something all wrong about a schoolyard without children playing, shouting, and running. He'd be glad when the school session started again in the fall. He always was.

Steven's thoughts drifted to his son. He remembered when Ethan was in grade school. In reality, it wasn't all that long ago—only six years—but it seemed longer. Ethan was becoming a man right before Steven's eyes. He was already an inch taller than Steven and still growing. His voice had lowered before he'd turned fourteen, and this year he'd started shaving regularly.

Cute enough to drive the girls crazy, Ethan was a serious student, carrying a four-point grade average. He was musically gifted and played several different instruments, all of them well. A theater buff, he'd starred in this spring's high school production of *A Midsummer Night's Dream*. Like all the Welbys, Ethan was athletically inclined, although he preferred sports like golf, tennis, and swimming to the rowdier team sports favored by his dad and uncles.

And now, thanks to the generosity of Dallas and Paula Hurst, Ethan was about to become the owner of a classic '55 Chevy.

Steven grinned. His son would never suspect. It was no secret he wanted to own a car, but he'd been saving the money he earned at his part-time job for college. Everybody expected him to get a scholarship, of course, but Ethan was smart enough to know there would be plenty of other out-of-pocket expenses. He said he'd rather borrow his mom's car or ride his bike than come up short of cash when it came time for college.

That was one of the reasons Dallas had insisted on buying the car. "How many boys Ethan's age are that levelheaded?" he'd asked Steven last week. "Maybe you were, but I wasn't. I'm lucky I graduated at all."

Steven turned his chair toward his desk, his thoughts progressing in a different direction.

Dallas never had said why he and Paula didn't have children of their own after nearly nine years of marriage—whether by choice or because they couldn't—and Steven never had asked. As close as the two couples were, that was one subject that seemed off-limits. Steven couldn't say why. It just was.

What he knew for certain was this—Dallas would make a great dad.

~

Paula Hurst honored Gerard Stone with one of her most dazzling smiles as she shook his hand. "I certainly appreciate your time, Mr. Stone. I'll look forward to hearing the bank's decision by the end of the week."

"Always a pleasure, Ms. Hurst." His admiring gaze was most definitely *not* businesslike. "I promise not to keep you waiting." He picked up his briefcase and headed for the office door. "Perhaps I'll deliver the news in person, if I happen to be in the neighborhood."

Paula followed him, said another polite farewell, then closed the door behind him. Immediately, a shudder passed through her. "The old lecher," she whispered. But she would do a lot to swing this deal for Henry & Associates, even flirt with that obnoxious gray-haired banker.

Paula walked toward the ceiling-to-floor windows that formed the north wall of her office. She looked first at the panoramic view of the mountains, the foothill grasses green in these early days of June. Then her gaze dropped to the busy downtown street fifteen stories below. The rush hour traffic was in full swing.

She glanced at her wristwatch. She was supposed to meet Dallas for supper at *Billet Doux*, the new French restaurant that was all the rage. Since her meeting with the boorish Mr. Stone had taken longer than expected, she would have to skip her gym session if she wanted to make their reservation.

She sighed. What she needed was about ten more hours in her day and one extra day in her week. Maybe then she could get everything done.

She turned to her desk, punched a key on her telephone, and waited for her assistant to answer.

"Yes, Ms. Hurst?"

"Myra, please call my trainer and tell her I'll need to reschedule for tomorrow." She glanced at her pocket PC, already open in her hand. "See if she's available around eleven. Otherwise, I'll have to call her back. Oh, and would you remind me to pick up my dry cleaning on Wednesday."

"I'll take care of it."

"Thanks, Myra. See you in the morning."

"Good night."

Paula walked into the private washroom connected to her office. She checked her makeup, put on fresh lipstick, and ran a pick through her hair. Then she stepped back from the mirror to assess her appearance.

She'd turned thirty last winter, but she didn't look it. She didn't carry one ounce of unwanted fat. In fact, she was at least five pounds thinner than the day she graduated from high school. She smiled, remembering the wolf whistles she'd received the last time she visited the Overland Resort construction site. Come to think of it, her husband had been known to whistle at her a time or two himself.

How she loved the way Dallas loved her. He lavished her with gifts, spoiled her rotten, took her on romantic vacations to exotic places. True, he was disappointed they didn't have children, but that just meant he could love her more. She was perfectly content to be the center of his life.

She flicked off the washroom light and returned to her desk, where she retrieved her purse from the bottom drawer, then left the office.

It was a pleasant evening, warm but not hot, and *Billet Doux* was only three blocks from the Henry & Associates office complex. Paula decided to walk rather than taking her car from the parking garage. Maybe, she thought, the short stroll would partially make up for her missed workout.

As she approached the restaurant, she recognized Dallas, seated at one of the outdoor tables. A waitress was standing near him, smiling, laughing . . . blushing. Her husband often had that effect on women. Ruggedly handsome with thick black hair and deep-set brown eyes—"bedroom eyes" was how a friend of Paula's described them—Dallas Hurst was a living, breathing definition of sex appeal. He had a warm, easy laugh, and when he was with a woman, he gave her his full attention. Who wouldn't find *that* attractive?

Arriving at the entrance to the patio, Paula shot the waitress a hostile glance, then sweetly said, "Hi, handsome."

Dallas looked in her direction, smiled, and rose from his chair. "Hey, beautiful."

The waitress left.

"Have you been waiting long?" Paula entered the small fenced patio through the gate.

"Only long enough to order a drink. Want anything?"

"Just water," she answered.

He pulled out a chair from the table, waiting for her to be seated. "You don't mind if we eat outside, do you? It's a perfect evening for it."

"No, I don't mind. I walked here for the same reason."

Before she sat down, she rose up on tiptoe and kissed him. "How was your afternoon?"

He chuckled, his expression sheepish. "I talked Steve into letting me drive the Chevy over to his brother's place. That's where they're hiding it until the party." He shrugged. "I took the long route getting there, and by the time I got a cab back to the dealer's, I figured there wasn't much point in going to the plant. So I did some shopping instead." He reached for his jacket, lying over the back of another chair, and pulled a small gold box from the pocket. He slid it toward her on the table. "Thanks for going along with buying the car for Ethan."

Paula scarcely heard his final words as she lifted the lid from the box. Inside was a platinum-and-diamond necklace.

"Dallas, it's exquisite." She met his gaze. "I love it." She leaned forward, taking hold of his hand. "And I love you."

~

Later that night, Dallas lay in bed, listening to Paula's contented breathing as she slept, nestled close to his side, her head resting on his shoulder. But sleep escaped him, and he knew why. He'd meant to tell Paula about his visit to Dr. Kramer. All evening long he'd planned to tell her, but the right moment had eluded him as surely as sleep did now.

He pressed his face close to Paula's head and breathed in the sweet fragrance of her hair.

Dallas didn't know why he hadn't told her he was going to see the doctor. Maybe because she seemed so sensitive whenever he brought up the subject of children. But wasn't it better to know *why* they didn't have kids after all these years?

They had a good marriage. They were successful in their respective businesses. Their combined income was a generous six figures. Dallas would be forty-one in less than two months, and Paula was thirty. It was time they had children.

But first they needed to know if they *could* have children. He'd taken the first step by seeing Dr. Kramer. The news he'd received today was good. There was nothing wrong with him. No reason he couldn't father children. So now he had to convince Paula to go in for a few tests herself. She wasn't going to like that. She hated doctors and needles and hospitals and tests of any kind.

This was going to take special handling.